"Allow the words of this gem to elevate you to the royal position God has placed you because God is your King, and you are God's child. This book will lovingly take you through a journey of dismantling spiritual roadblocks to enjoying freedom once you fully surrender to God. Come out of hiding and into your God-given purpose with *Experience Greater: An Intimate Journey with God*."
—Stephanie Thomas, Ph.D., *Thomas Teacher Prep*

PRAISE FOR *EXPERIENCING GREATER:*

"Dr. Richardson invites the reader to embrace, move and grow with God in new ways. This wonderfully written story reminds the reader that spiritual transformation is available to all when we journey with God. If you want your life to be spiritually transformed and you are ready to move to the next level in your spiritual journey, I highly recommend you read this book!"

—Vikki T. Gaskin-Butler, M.Div., Ph.D.,

Psychologist/clergy

"Reading this book was an experience. It had so many twists and turns, and every part was relatable. The characters resonated with me and it TRULY, TRULY blessed me! It is a masterpiece."

—Minister Bryan Williams

"Spiritual freedom requires you to remain in a consistent state of surrender. In *Experiencing Greater*, Dr. Richardson weaves a moving story of spiritual freedom and personal growth. Her protagonist, Royalty, desperately wants to understand and embrace her progression and conversion while on an unknowing journey toward a higher spiritual level. Royalty is detoxing her soul to allow in the transformative presence of Mighty God, ultimately sharing thirty-one combined lessons from her spiritually emerged self, and other inspirational forces along her journey. This book is a must-read!"

—Portia York, Ph.D., *York Creative Education Group*

"I know many people who *need* to read this book, though they may not like reading the truth about themselves and why they're stuck in mediocrity. They're just like the main character, Royalty. They attack and blame the very person sent to help them, and believe they're right to do so. This book is nuanced and plain at the same time. It takes insights from the Bible and fleshes them out so we can *see* what those scriptural tidbits really mean in our lives. The way it is written, we can understand exactly why the main character is uncomfortable during her journey, and why she's wrong not to trust her spiritual guide, the Driver."

—Reverend Vicky Lee, M.Div.,
Pastor, Hale Ho'onani A.M.E. Church, Hawai'i

Experiencing Greater

An Intimate Journey with God

Sonyia Richardson, Ph.D.

ANOTHER LEVEL PRESS
Charlotte, North Carolina

Another Level Press / Sonyia Richardson
SonyiaRichardson.com

Disclaimer: This is a work of fiction. All characters are products of the author's imagination and are not to be construed as real. Any resemblance to actual people, living or dead, or to businesses, companies, events, institutions, or locales is completely coincidental.

Copy editing and book production Stephanie Gunning
Cover design by Gus Yoo

Library of Congress Control Number 2023905058

Experiencing Greater / Sonyia Richardson — 1st ed.

ISBN 979-8-9875856-0-3 (paperback)

To my spouse, children, siblings, parents, and other amazing ancestors.

CONTENTS

PREFACE

Have you ever been in hiding? Not because some-one was searching for you and you didn't want to be found. But because you were afraid to show up fully in the world. I have.

The concept for this book was given to me by my dear friend Minister Bryan Williams. When he told me one day, "You are like royalty living in peasant clothes," I had no idea what he meant, so he patiently spent the next few minutes explaining it to me. I experienced an immediate awakening: I was living beneath my calling and trying to be invisible or hide. I was trying to fit in, but it wasn't working. I was not showing up as my authentic self, but as a mediocre version of myself, afraid to be great. And it wasn't working well for me. He could see that I was limiting myself from my God-given purpose.

As a result of accepting that I had lived most of my life in hiding and was honestly afraid to let the world see me fully show up, I went forward into the next year with a new theme for my life: "I am that I am." I now believed that to understand who I was, I must understand the entire identity of God and how it was being reflected in me. The subsequent year focused on knowing and accepting my identity and allowing myself to exist in all my greatness. I committed to coming out of hiding.

Incidentally, it was around this time that I was given a vision for this book. I initially resisted writing it because I knew it would push me out of my comfort zone. More would be required of me. My journey of learning to show up required that I also learn to surrender.

Surrendering is a complicated process, and in writing this book, I often stopped for months at a time. There was much to learn, and I sometimes needed to wait to hear what to do directly from God. I also waited because my understanding, image, and perception of the identity of the Divine were being disrupted. To fully know myself, I had to strengthen my relationship with God.

Essentially, writing this book was a spiritual process, like a detox for my soul. As you read the pages, you may experience similar moments of awakening and release.

Ideas in this book were generated partially by listening to the sermons of my pastor Rev. Dr.

Franklin D. Watkins of Oak Grove Baptist Church in Harrisburg, North Carolina. I am grateful to my church family for their prayers. I also thank Rev. Jordan Boyd, who has supported my work and is a co-laborer in helping to heal others emotionally and psychologically.

This writing process took at least four years to complete as I had to go through a refining process. Year one focused on gaining an understanding of the identity of God. By the end of year two, I realized that my knowledge of the identity of God was being expanded.

During year three, I accepted that the God I was now worshipping was different from the God I had been raised to worship. I had to fight and resist the image of God taught me by my early church, which was a God of punishment and judgment. I learned that God had compassion for me and truly cared about justice. I no longer limited my understanding of God to a masculine being but realized that, as a spirit, God can exist in a myriad of identities. Knowing this, I realized I needed to fully surrender and trust God.

During year four, I implemented the life theme of withholding nothing and was at a point in my life where I agreed that I would no longer withhold any of my gifts, greatness, and purpose. I was no longer withholding because I understood the identity of the God I served.

I also experienced a life situation that caused me to insert additional content into the book. As a result, I added the chapter on how to avoid being led away from the path and purpose the Divine has directed for me. Despite others stating that this was the path God wanted me to walk, I had to listen and follow the Divine's still, small voice. I had to acknowledge that God does not explicitly favor persons but instead speaks directly to me the same way God speaks to others. I am grateful the Divine allowed me to go through this experience to write about it and inspire others.

Finally, I want to thank my family, who have supported every goal I pursued. Thanks for your support and unconditional love for me. You have made me stronger and more confident, and I thank you for your investment in my life. I'm grateful to my parents, Linwood and Vernell Copeland, who instilled in me a commitment to spirituality, a relationship with God, and a love for family. And a special thanks to my siblings, Victor, L.C., and Triva, who have taught me that success and purpose don't fit into a neatly wrapped box.

A special thanks to my husband, Rondell Richardson, and our two sons, Micah and Jayson. Thanks for your love!

CHAPTER 1

Royalty in Peasant Clothes

Once upon a time, a woman named Royalty lived in a large, overcrowded metropolitan region. Her city, Peasantville, was home to the country's largest population of peasants, people who led simple, mediocre, unfulfilling lives. Like her friends and neighbors, Royalty generally settled for average and rarely pursued lofty goals. A modest life was the standard for the peasants in town.

Everything in the town was unexceptional. The streets were rugged and narrow, but travelable. The buildings were old, tiny, and dirty, but habitable. The businesses were numerous, but not too profitable or sustainable. There was a low unemployment rate, but the peasants were underpaid, so they lived modestly. The politicians were busy, but the town's policies were not impactful. The schools operated year-round, but the students were not academically thriving. The hospitals had access to personnel, facilities, and equipment, but people were not healed. The services of different faith communities were filled weekly with peasants, but no one was transformed. Everything was in a state of mere existence.

And the peasants were pleased with this state of affairs. They were comfortable with it because they felt like they had everything they needed. They were satisfied with only having their basic needs met.

Despite Peasantville being such an average and unimpressive town, it was the gold standard for the rest of the country. Others sought to duplicate conditions there.

Royalty was comfortable living in Peasantville. As a peasant, she spoke like a peasant, dressed like a peasant, and functioned like a peasant. Royalty fully embraced this as her identity.

As a people, the peasants tended to be self-centered and individualistic. They worked hard to safeguard their limited possessions. There was little to no sharing of resources, and they were not concerned about the needs of their neighbors.

Because of this self-serving mentality, they settled for mediocrity and were completely satisfied with the limited materials and success they obtained and achieved.

Low Expectations

Although the town was full of peasants, unfortunately, some people in the city were discriminated against simply because of their family name. This was the case for the Jones family, of which Royalty was a member. The Joneses were despised and ranked as having the lowest social status in the town. They had no control over this designation, which was frustrating, as there was no meaningful justification for their status being so low. However, some rumors circulated that, generations before, several members of the family had left Peasantville and never returned. To leave Peasantville was considered blasphemy, as this was supposed to be the "best town" in the country. Anyone who left immediately became an outsider.

Royalty's family had never confirmed or denied the rumors that some of their relatives had left town, and she herself had never known anyone who had left Peasantville.

Despite what others thought of her, Royalty excelled at being mediocre and self-serving. She believed, like the other peasants, that the purpose of her life was to be comfortable and avoid distress by any means. Daily, Royalty dedicated herself to being the best peasant she could be. She believed she could live her best life if she worked a little harder than the other peasants despite enduring discrimination and prejudice that others weren't experiencing.

Royalty wore regular peasant clothes. These were basic and only existed in solid colors. There were no patterns, floral designs, unique stitching, or embroidering. The solid colors were all darker tones, including blue, green, black, and brown. The clothes were discounted, baggy, and made with polyester fabric. Because they were cheaply made, they were not expected to last longer than a year or so.

The peasants worshipped God but had super low expectations for him. Accordingly, they rarely operated outside of their comfort zones and never believed they needed to. They were proud of their simple and inconsistent prayers and faith. They expected God to answer their simple prayers and leave them alone otherwise. Their view of God was minor, and so was their faith.

Strangely enough, most people believed God favored the peasants of higher social ranks even though their lives were quite similar to everyone else's. Royalty did not hold this particular belief—in fact, she refused to believe that God preferred one group of peasants over another. To her, this represented foolish, ignorant thinking. Her prayer was that God would remove the oppression and discrimination faced by her family and change the townspeople's beliefs about them.

Royalty grew in her peasant faith and was active in her religious place of worship. She felt sure that God was well pleased with her. She tried to make decisions that closely adhered to her morals and values. She knew she had favor because whenever she prayed, her prayers were answered. It was super easy for Royalty to maintain her faith as she had learned to pray for just enough and to expect only a little.

Approached by a Stranger

Early one cool and crisp October morning, Royalty took her usual morning walk in the neighborhood. She wasn't one to notice the fresh air, green trees, or blue skies. She could, however, hear her breathing and noticed herself wheezing when she climbed the big hills on the street. As she walked up an avenue, she saw a matte black, box-shaped older car with a damaged hood following her along her route. She turned and went down a side street to evade it and saw that the car continued to follow her. It slowly pulled up beside her. The driver slowly eased down the driver's side window.

Through the open window, Royalty noticed an immaculately dressed stranger behind the wheel. She had never seen someone dressed like her before. Although they seemed about the same age, the stranger presented herself in a very different manner. This woman had on a bright pink brimmed hat and wore her hair pulled back in a ponytail. She also wore a bold, floral-patterned dress and had red lipstick painted on her lips, red blush on her cheeks, and black shades covering her eyes.

The driver paused to look Royalty up and down, but she said nothing.

"Hi, can I help you with something?" Royalty asked the driver.

"Well, I don't need help, but I do have an important message for you. You are the next peasant assigned to leave Peasantville. This is an assignment for you and an appointed purpose. You are being called to pursue greater things, but you must have a willing spirit before you can leave. Many are invited, but only a special few accept the invitation," said the driver.

Royalty mumbled under her breath, "This doesn't make any sense." Then she asked herself a series of questions that she figured weren't going to be answered by this stranger. *Why is she speaking so foolishly? Is she drunk? On drugs? Did she get lost?* One thing she knew for sure was that the stranger wasn't a peasant—because if she were a peasant, she would have known that there could be no place greater to be than Peasantville.

Royalty's thoughts were interrupted by the stranger, who spoke again. "One day, I will come back to pick you up so you can start your journey away from Peasantville for good. It will be important that you decide *right at that moment* to get in the car. And once you begin the ride, you should know that you need to have sufficient faith to finish the journey. This is a necessary journey for your life, so don't refuse the ride. Many people before you have refused to get in the car. And many who started the journey didn't make it to the end. However, I believe in you and know you are destined for more than this town has to offer. Because I care about you, I wanted to warn you directly: It will have dire consequences if you don't agree to hop in when invited."

Royalty said under her breath inaudibly, so the stranger couldn't hear her, "Who is this driver? And what does she really want from me? This is odd. Why should I get into a car with a stranger without knowing where I am going? How do I know this driver can be trusted?"

The stranger must have read Royalty's thoughts, as she immediately responded, "I understand your fears, but this car ride is about learning to trust the driver. You will be perfectly safe if you ride in the car. Life is average, but not magical, here in Peasantville, and average cannot coexist with signs, wonders, and miracles. All that is required is for you to hop into the car and ride."

Sensing Royalty's apprehensiveness, the stranger said her goodbye and quickly drove away. Royalty didn't fully understand their conversation, but she felt like either the stranger had confused her with someone else or was genuinely crazy. Why else would she expect Royalty to get in the car with a stranger with no clue of where they were going? Yes, this stranger had to be out of her mind.

Confusion Mounts

Days passed and Royalty continued ruminating about the conversation with the stranger. It kept replaying in her head and made her anxious. To ease her anxiety and rid herself of these crazy thoughts, Royalty sought wisdom from a local minister. He was a peasant but didn't fit in with the other peasants. He was often seen walking alone, not because he had no friends, but because he was particular about who received his time and attention. Royalty found the minister sitting under a giant oak tree brimming and budding with bonfire red and sun flame golden leaves. Royalty bent down and sat beside the minister and updated him about the conversation with the stranger.

Royalty chuckled to herself as she briefed him about the stranger's directive, "One day, a driver will come by to pick you up and attempt to drive you away from Peasantville. Just get in the car and ride. This is a necessary journey, don't refuse the ride. There will be dire consequences if you don't hop in."

"What exactly does this mean?" inquired Royalty, hoping that the peasant minister would have an explanation.

"Are you sure you are ready to find out the answer?" asked the peasant minister.

Surprised that there was more to the story, Royalty looked at the minister with sincerity and stated, "Yes, I'm ready."

"Once I share my answer with you, you will no longer be able to act as if you don't know. Your ignorance will be gone, and your spirit will be awakened. Royalty, I have shared this message with many other peasants before you, but most of them thought I was crazy and did not believe what I told them. If I share this information with you, it may have consequences for me as I could lose your support and friendship," said the minister.

Hearing the sadness in his voice, Royalty got a little frightened about what she was about to hear. At the same time, she had the highest level of respect for the minister and knew she would believe whatever he shared.

"Yes, I'm sure I'm ready. I value our friendship and your mentorship. I believe and trust the words you share and know that you have no intention to mislead me," answered Royalty.

They sat in silence for a few moments. Royalty could tell that the minister was contemplating his new move. Although she was eager for him to speak, she also wanted him to know that he could take his time and wait until he was ready. As she sat in momentary silence with the minister, she noticed the oak tree and its multicolored leaves for the first time. She also noticed the shade the tree provided them, shielding them from the sunlight. She saw the slight bend of the oak tree's trunk and its leaning toward the sun.

Her moments of mindfulness was interrupted by the minister explaining, "In life, not all caterpillars change into butterflies or moths. Some remain caterpillars, while others transform. But have you ever witnessed a caterpillar that remains a caterpillar, one that never transforms into a moth or butterfly? Would you even know if you saw it that it wouldn't change? No. We expect the caterpillar to go through metamorphosis if given the opportunity, and to welcome the opportunity to change."

Royalty listened attentively, attempting not to disturb his train of thought. But she needed additional clarity for this to make sense.

The minister continued, "Just like the caterpillar, you are attempting to remain a caterpillar. You are dressed like a peasant, talk like a peasant, and live like a peasant. But the peasant life is a life of limited growth and stagnation. It is the life of a caterpillar that doesn't want to grow into its potential. You have tried to blend in with the other peasants but were never supposed to remain a peasant."

"The day you let go of your peasant status and lifestyle will be the day that you begin your metamorphosis. However, this requires you to have the willingness to change and grow. This growth and change will require some periods of discomfort, but it also comes with signs, miracles, and wonders. Once you transform, you will become an example for all the other peasants. You were created for growth and transformation."

Royalty had a deep, hollow feeling in her stomach. Why would the minister encourage her to change? And why had he waited until now to reveal this? Royalty thought that his words might be a mistake. All she had ever known was her existence as a simple peasant. And the lifestyle was easy.

She made a connection to the myth shared around town about her family's history of leaving Peasantville. Could there be truth to the story? Would Royalty damage her family's name if she chose to leave like they did? None of her immediate family members had ever tried to be different from a peasant, though the myths suggest that her great-grandmother and great-grandfather left, and when they returned, they were never the same. Her immediate family learned from their history that it was best to conform. Her unsettled feeling started to grow deeper.

What if a better life was available? Similarly, what if that better life only lasted a few weeks or months? Royalty lay down under the oak tree and tried to eliminate her noisy thoughts. As she did, she observed the magnitude of the tree and how heavy its limbs were. She looked at the multicolored leaves on the tree and noticed how they were attached to the branches. Every minute or so, leaves would fall from the tree to the ground. But the leaves never drifted too far away from the tree.

At this point, Royalty was unsure what to say to the minister. Sensing her discomfort, he informed her that he was going to head back into the church. Royalty softly thanked him for his words and looked down as he walked away.

Now Royalty was even more confused. In an attempt to receive clarification and direction, she prayed. But she didn't feel the presence of God. "God should be able to clarify these revelations," she mumbled. Disappointed, Royalty tried again to pray but still didn't feel anything special. She was not ready to be anything different than a peasant and evidently unprepared to walk away from the comforts of Peasantville.

As much as she didn't want things to change, things were not feeling the same. Royalty grew disheartened and began to grieve her familiar peasant lifestyle. What once had felt like a lifestyle and land of excellence began to feel average. The familiar church where she worshipped no longer felt like an anchor. The comfort that Royalty had in this land was starting to dissipate.

Royalty now understood what the minister had meant when he told her that once she was informed about the problems, she would no longer be able to act as if she didn't know. She was sad and grieving her old lifestyle. She wanted to talk to her family members to discuss her experiences but believed they wouldn't understand. Royalty felt alone, like she was stranded on a desert island. Something was different, and things were changing without her consent.

CHAPTER 2

My Soul Says Yes

A few weeks later, the sunshine pouring through her bedroom window vividly beat down on Royalty's skin as she awakened to a new day. Usually, Royalty was grateful for the day and the new opportunities it brought her. Though the sun was shining, this day seemed different. Royalty pleaded to God for things to return to how they had been, but she couldn't feel his presence and did not get a response. She was beginning to grow more and more frustrated. This new lifestyle of waiting for more wasn't giving Royalty the same joy as before.

Attempting to make the best of the day, Royalty got dressed and went for her morning walk. Surely the exercise would help her feel better.

Just as Royalty began the first of her customary 10,000 steps, she noticed a familiar matte black, box-shaped car pull up alongside her. The driver slowly rolled down the window and greeted Royalty as if they were long-lost friends. She had a massive smile on her face and was wearing a salmon-colored dress and an apple green baseball cap.

"Good morning, Royalty," the driver said. "I'm here to pick you up and take you on a journey."

"Where are we going?" asked Royalty, this time having the courage and mental wherewithal to ask additional questions.

"On a journey," the driver repeated without offering further explanation.

Royalty grew even more suspicious and leery of the driver. The driver seemed nonthreatening and cordial. Still, Royalty didn't trust her. Royalty informed the driver she would pass on the ride and instead returned home immediately. She was unwilling to leave her place of peace and comfort, especially if she didn't understand what she was exchanging it for.

Weeks passed and Royalty no longer fit in at work, home, and church. She no longer felt the presence of God when she prayed. And the goals that Royalty once had no longer excited her. She was bored with her mundane peasant lifestyle. It was not working.

The only thing that excited Royalty anymore was her relationship with the peasant minister. The messages he was sharing with her were profound. He advised her by speaking indirectly, in parables. He proclaimed himself a prophet and didn't hold anything back. Because Royalty appreciated the minister's transparency and trusted his counsel, she decided to pay him another visit. Something had to be done to regain some of her former joy.

She met the minister under the oak tree again. He smiled as he saw Royalty coming towards him. "You decided to return," he said in a surprised tone as if he had never expected to see Royalty again.

"Yeah, I didn't feel as if I had a choice. You are the only person I can talk to about what is happening in my life. Everyone else would think that I am losing it if I said something. They would also look for the black car intending to steer the driver out of town. My family would not want their name ever associated again with a peasant who leaves town," stated Royalty.

"I'm sure yours is a difficult situation to be in," said the minister. But I also want you to understand how much of a blessing it is. Many are called, but few are chosen."

"But do I have to be the chosen one?" complained Royalty.

"Favor can be seen as a burden until you accept it as a blessing," stated the minister.

"But favor shouldn't make my current life miserable, should it?" inquired Royalty.

"Your life makes you miserable now because you are no longer comfortable. Favor is uprooting you from accepting average as the status quo, which no longer brings you contentment. Your spirit is longing for more," said the minister. "The only way you will find contentment and joy again is to leave. You were meant for more, Royalty."

"But what about my family? I can't leave them behind," Royalty whined.

"You're not leaving them behind. Many of your ancestors already made this journey," the minister said.

Hearing this, Royalty finally began to understand. Perhaps there was some truth to the myths she'd heard about her family.

"How certain are you of that?" inquired Royalty.

"Because I come from a family of ministers. Your ancestors always consulted with my ancestors regarding the journey. Our purpose was simply to help them build the faith and trust to accept the ride in the car when the invitation came. Some of your current family members were also asked to take the ride and lacked the courage to take it. They were more obedient to their family than to their purpose," explained the minister patiently.

"How can I trust that I am supposed to take this ride?" asked Royalty, hoping the minister didn't have a complete answer.

"Because your name is Royalty. You were never designed to be a peasant," the minister responded with a smile. "Your questions indicate that the work of getting ready to leave has already begun. The beginning of the journey can be painful as you lose your excitement and joy for what used to exist. The things you used to do and have can no longer satisfy you. You have already taken the first step of your journey without realizing it," he said.

Royalty wanted to return the minister's smile but was too unhappy. She didn't realize she had already consented to go on the journey.

"The day you visited me, and I prophesized to you about your destiny," said the peasant minister, "was the day you said yes. Your spirit whispered a yes to the oak tree. When you lay under it, you were laying down your need to control everything. You surrendered at that moment. You learned to trust the tree, and the tree helped you to calm your mind."

"Now that you mention it, lying under the tree was rather calming. But how did you know that my spirit had whispered yes under the tree?" inquired Royalty.

"I knew your spirit whispered yes because I heard it. I heard the rustling of the leaves and the blowing of the wind," stated the peasant minister. "The trees celebrate every time someone says yes. If you listen closely, you will hear the trees celebrating today's victories."

Royalty was already feeling at peace within herself. She had always believed she had the support of the peasant minister, but now felt relieved to know that she had the support of nature as well, including the trees. This was something new.

"As the trees begin to celebrate your yes, doors and opportunities will open. Keep your eyes and heart open for these new opportunities," the peasant minister stated.

"So, speaking of new opportunities, well, ugh … a black car pulled up beside me a couple of weeks ago in my neighborhood. An odd-looking woman was inside the car and invited me to get in, but I refused. Do you think I missed my chance to take this journey?" asked Royalty, beginning to put together the pieces.

"The driver was testing you to see if you would be obedient," replied the peasant minister. "And testing if you were ready to leave Peasantville and enter new territory. Your response to the driver let her know that you weren't ready yet," explained the minister.

"When will the driver return?" asked Royalty.

"I'm not certain she will," replied the peasant minister. "There is no guarantee. She has other peasants whom she is seeking to liberate."

Saddened by this news, Royalty became solemn and reflected on the previous few months. *What if I never have this opportunity again? Will I be miserable in Peasantville forever? My happiness and joy are gone.*

And apparently, my spirit consented to all this while I was sitting under an old oak tree. Royalty shook her head in disbelief.

Royalty began to long for a different life away from Peasantville. She was daydreaming about the driver coming back to pick her up and take her far away to another land. Her spirit had already said yes, and now Royalty's heart was starting to say the same. Royalty accepted how the moment of surrender under the oak tree awakened her spiritual eyes, enabling her to notice the bondage of life in Peasantville. This entire population existed in the bondage of mediocrity. But Royalty refused to remain in this bondage anymore and was determined to find a way to escape.

CHAPTER 3

Back Seat, Please

About two winters, springs, summers, and falls later, Royalty was again taking her morning walk through her neighborhood. She had again grown accustomed to life in Peasantville. She still had not found her joy, but she had learned how to tolerate the mediocrity of the town. She had maintained her silence about the incident with the driver the whole time and had avoided speaking with the minister at church since they discussed it. She accepted that she had likely missed her opportunity for the journey. She continued to contemplate ways to escape Peasantville and dreamed about it often.

During her daily walks, Royalty was on the lookout for dark cars riding through her neighborhood, hoping the black car would return and the driver invite her to take a ride again. But it had been more than two years, and neither the stranger nor the car had returned. Royalty began to lose hope.

On this day, in the corner of her eye, Royalty noticed a Carolina blue car driving slowly through the neighborhood. She had never seen this car before, so it looked rather suspicious. She sped up, thinking she might need to get back home in case anything weird was about to happen. She turned left at the first corner and raced down the sidewalk.

The car was now following her and had sped up slightly as well. The vehicle approached Royalty and came to a complete stop. Royalty's heart was racing with anxiety. Should she run or stay and get whatever was coming to her? Before making a final decision, the passenger side window rolled down, and the driver said to Royalty, "I'm back."

The voice sounded familiar, and Royalty realized she was staring into the eyes of the same driver who had offered her the ride in the black car two years earlier. This time though, the driver was wearing a hoodie, jogging pants, and a baseball cap. She had taupe gloss on her lips and pearl earrings in her ears. Before the driver could say anything else, Royalty grasped the handle on the front passenger side door and pulled the door open. She sat down in the passenger seat with a massive grin and greeted the driver. She wasn't going to let this opportunity pass her by and knew she must get it right this time.

"I am so glad you gave me a second chance," Royalty exclaimed.

She was caught off guard when the driver demanded, "Back seat, please." The driver didn't appear excited at all that she had climbed into the car this time.

Royalty apprehensively got out and then entered the car's back seat and closed the door. She wondered why the driver was so rude. *Didn't she come back to pick me up? Doesn't she realize she needs me as I am a chosen peasant? The driver must not realize who I am,* Royalty thought to herself. *I'll have to tell her how good of a peasant I am.*

Royalty expected the driver to be happy that she'd decided to get into the car this time. However, this wasn't being celebrated or even acknowledged. The driver didn't say another word, only pulled away from the curb quickly and began maneuvering in and out of traffic. The driver hurriedly left Peasantville, but Royalty had no clue where they were going. She only wondered why the driver felt the need to leave Peasantville so hurriedly. *Are we fleeing from something or someone?*

Royalty began to second guess herself and wondered if she should have left Peasantville after all. But in her heart, she knew it was time for a change. She decided to deal with the rudeness of the driver by ignoring her for most of the trip. She wanted to focus on getting to the final destination.

Warning Signs

Royalty noticed the quietness in the car. The driver wasn't talking, no music was playing, and she couldn't hear any air coming out of the vents. It was such an awkward silence.

The driver kept her head focused forward, eased the car past the outskirts of Peasantville, and entered a small rural town.

Suddenly, Royalty was startled by a loud, rumbling noise from the front of the car. The driver slowly pulled over to the emergency stopping lane. The driver didn't get out of the car to check the engine. She just sat in her seat and waited.

Unsure of what was happening, Royalty asked the driver, "Are you going to check the engine?"

"No," stated the driver. "We just have to sit here and wait."

They sat and waited. Five minutes. Ten minutes. Twenty minutes. The driver never called anyone to let them know they were stuck.

Finally, in her restlessness, Royalty inquired, "Aren't you going to do something?"

The driver shook her head and softly whispered, "Wait."

Royalty waited for another twenty minutes before she had finally had enough. At this point, the road was empty, and few cars were passing them. "I can't do this," she mumbled under her breath. If this were what happened within the first two hours of the trip, she couldn't imagine being on the road with this driver for days. Perhaps she had the wrong driver. Maybe she needed someone a little more competent.

Deciding to fix the problem herself, Royalty told the driver, "I'm going to get out and walk back to Peasantville."

"That's fine," replied the driver.

Frustrated by what appeared to be the driver's lack of concern about addressing their situation, Royalty swung the back door open, hopped out, and slammed the door shut behind her. Headed in the direction from which they came, Royalty began her long walk home. Royalty could see Peasantville in the distance, but it looked very far away. By now, the sun was setting and the sky was beginning to get darker. There was no way Royalty would make it back home walking. And she wasn't comfortable enough to try to catch a ride with another stranger. About half a mile from the car, Royalty got discouraged and dropped to her knees.

"Why did I ever leave home?" Royalty muttered. "Things were just so much easier in Peasantville."

Royalty debated whether she should continue walking back to Peasantville or turning around and getting back in the car with the driver. In desperation, she called out to God, but then she quickly remembered that he hadn't been answering her prayers for a couple of years. Royalty felt like there was only one real option.

CHAPTER 4

The City of Fear

Royalty returned to the Carolina blue car and jumped into the back seat without saying a word. The driver was patiently sitting in the driver's seat as if she were expecting Royalty to return. As they continued to sit there in silence, Royalty was growing more accustomed to it.

Approximately fifteen minutes later, the driver opened her door and exited the car. Royalty watched through the window as the driver reached into the trunk and reappeared with a five-quart container of motor oil. Lifting the hood, the driver pulled out the car's dipstick, wiped it off, and then reinserted it to check the oil. The driver then added fresh oil to the oil fill port and rechecked the level with the dipstick. The driver closed the lid, walked around to the back of the car, put the empty container in the trunk, wiped her hands on a cloth, and then reentered the car. The driver calmly turned the key to start the vehicle, and the engine immediately revved.

Royalty was grateful but irritated. She wondered why the driver hadn't fixed the car hours earlier. Within minutes, they were back on the road, moving further away from Peasantville. *She is trying my patience*, Royalty thought to herself irritably.

The car drove down the road. In the backseat, Royalty was growing weary from the day's events. She leaned against the window and rested her head. She closed both eyes and drifted into a deep sleep.

Darkness Looms

Several hours later, Royalty was awakened by soft classical music playing in the background. She was a little disoriented and fatigued but remembers being in the car with the stranger. *So, this isn't a dream*, she thought. She looked outside the window but couldn't see anything as it was entirely dark outside. The only lights noticeable were beaming from their car.

"Where are we?" Royalty asked the driver, beginning to panic as she didn't see any landmarks, signs, or other vehicles.

"We are going through the City of Fear," stated the driver.

Goosebumps rose on Royalty's arms as the darkness engulfed their car. She began to doubt her decision to leave Peasantville and was growing tenser by the moment. The music on the radio seemed to grow louder and louder too. Royalty wanted to jump out of the car but worried because there was no sign of life. Instead of fleeing, she began to cry.

Royalty attempted to hide her tears from the driver. She didn't want to be perceived as weak. Her fear continued to intensify. Eventually, the hairs on Royalty's neck were at full attention. She remembered experiencing a similarly intense fear when she was nine years old, riding in the back seat of the car with her family. It was dark outside and the family was returning from her uncle's house. She also remembered being awakened by a large, crashing sound and the car swirling in circles.

Later she would learn that her family's car had been hit head on by a drunk driver who was being chased by the police. The drunk driver had lost control of his car, crossed the median, and directly hit theirs. Luckily, Royalty's family had walked away from that accident with minimal injury. So did the drunk driver, who disappeared into the woods and was never found. That same intense fear was returning on her current trip.

Anxious thoughts begin to spiral in Royalty's mind. *What if I don't make it out alive? What if the people in Peasantville are looking for me? What if I never make it back home?* These were interrupted by the humming of the driver. *Why is the driver so calm and peaceful? What is wrong with this driver?* Royalty wondered.

The more anxious thoughts Royalty had, the louder the driver's humming became. The humming ultimately was so loud that Royalty could no longer focus on her thoughts. Instead, she focused on the humming. Royalty began to hear a melody in the driver's humming. Once she did, an extraordinary, unexplainable peace instantly overtook her. Her body relaxed and she momentarily escaped all the worries, fears, and ideas that had been troubling her. As Royalty attended to the humming then, she noticed the volume was decreasing, and eventually, it had become a still, small voice.

The voice was repeating a mantra over and over.

"You keep in perfect peace those whose minds stay on you because they trust you."

Royalty reflected on these words. She was experiencing peace. Her mind was focused on the humming. However, she still couldn't say that she trusted the driver.

Usually, in moments of confusion like this, Royalty would pray; however, she believed that God had not been listening to her peasant prayers lately. So, she decided just to pray authentically, hoping God would be listening to her this time as a person, not just a peasant.

"Thank you for your peace," Royalty prayed. "Even though we're driving through a town named Fear, I'm living peacefully. Please help me to get safely to the final destination. By the way, thank you for my second chance to take the journey. Amen."

Royalty hoped God would hear her prayer and answer her this time.

She glanced at the driver's image reflected in the rearview mirror and noticed a slight smile on the driver's face. *What is she so happy about?* Royalty thought to herself.

Looking out the window, Royalty noticed a giant billboard about a mile up the street illuminated by bright lights in the dark sky.

"Yes!" Royalty exclaimed, "we are finally returning to civilization."

Royalty was getting accustomed to talking to herself as the driver provided only limited responses. As the car approached the billboard, Royalty was eager to discover what was on the sign. *Maybe it's an advertisement for a local restaurant,* she thought. Royalty's stomach had begun growling, but she didn't have time to notice.

As the car approached the billboard, Royalty could read the words aloud: I AM THAT I AM—MIGHTY GOD. Royalty quickly scanned the rest of the billboard, as she "knew" there must be more to the message. But there was nothing more. *That was weird,* she thought to herself. *What could that mean: I am that I am?* This was the first time Royalty had heard those words, or seen the name Mighty God. *Perhaps this is the god that the people in this area pray to,* she thought. *Maybe I should start directing my prayers to Mighty God as well.*

Prepared for the Journey

Realizing that there were no signs of restaurants in this area, Royalty settled into the back seat and listened to the grumbling in her stomach. Royalty asked the driver if they would encounter any restaurants or grocery stores on their journey. Instead of providing a verbal response, the driver reached down on the passenger side floor and handed Royalty a small, white paper bag.

"I made this, especially for you. It's your favorite," the driver matter-of-factly said.

Royalty doubted the driver knew her favorite foods but thanked her for the warm gesture. Feeling famished, she then opened the paper bag and was happy to find in it a chicken salad croissant, a cup of fruit, and a bottle of her favorite green tea. Everything she loved! As she was eating, Royalty reflected on how the driver had guessed or known what she liked. Maybe this food was what the driver liked to eat as well.

Royalty savored each bite of food. This had to be the absolute best chicken salad croissant she had ever had. And the fruit was so fresh and included all her favorites: watermelon, cantaloupe, grapes, and strawberries. Royalty washed everything down with the green tea, which had just the right touch of sweetness.

As Royalty finished the meal, she noticed thousands of tiny lights up ahead. It looked like they were approaching another city. She was relieved that the City of Fear was finally behind her.

She looked outside the window and deeply reflected on what she had learned so far on her journey and in the City of Fear.

1. *Fear is an emotion or feeling caused by the belief that something will not work out. It's important to identify the fears with which you are consumed.*

2. *The minister's prophecy to Royalty about taking the journey had helped her build the courage and desire to leave Peasantville.*

3. *She learned that when she was ready to quit and go back to Peasantville, it wasn't as easy as it seemed. When venturing off on an unfamiliar journey, there may be the desire to return to what is familiar. However, once you start the journey, it's challenging to go back to the status quo.*

4. *The driver had the resources and ability to fix the car but seemed to be waiting for Royalty to develop patience and trust before she used them. The driver fixed the car in her own time.*

5. *When dealing with fear, it is helpful to distract oneself. The humming from the driver helped to take Royalty's mind off her anxious thoughts.*

6. *Meditating on the powerful words "You keep in perfect peace those whose minds stay on you because they trust you," helped Royalty to increase her peace. Find a mantra or uplifting verse to focus on and repeat when dealing with fear and doubt.*

7. *The driver drove through the City of Fear and experienced no fear, doubt, or worry. It is possible to be in an area or time of your life that is scary and unknown, yet be free from fear, doubt, and worry. The driver was able to share her peace through humming. Learn how you can share your peace with others.*

CHAPTER 5

The City of Limitations

Royalty saw a small green road sign beside the highway. White lettering on the sign read: LIMITATIONS CITY LIMITS.

"That's weird," Royalty said aloud, "Who would name their town Limitations?" She chuckled to herself as the driver continued steering toward the city lights.

The darkness remained on the highway, but the headlights of the other cars shining on the roadway made it a little brighter. Once inside the City of Limitations, there were ample headlights from cars headed in both directions.

As dawn broke, the city was coming alive. Royalty could see that the streets were lined with familiar-looking hotels, gas stations, and restaurants. She hoped her driver would pull over and let her rest at a local hotel. But the driver picked up speed instead and appeared to be rapidly passing through the city. The driver sped past the exits.

Royalty leaned forward and tapped the driver on the shoulder. "Can we check into one of the hotels off the exit? I'm exhausted and need some rest," she said.

"I appreciate you asking for what you need, but no," the driver responded. "You don't want to stay in this town. We are headed to a great city."

"But I am so tired," said Royalty, "and I need some rest. The town reminds me of Peasantville. Can we stay, please?" she begged.

The driver reluctantly slowed down and veered the car towards the next exit.

On the local streets, Royalty was overwhelmed by the beauty of the city. The town looked relatively new, and the buildings extravagant. Royalty spotted a small boutique hotel about a block from the highway off-ramp and directed the driver to it. The driver pulled up to the front door of the hotel and allowed Royalty to exit the car. Royalty went to the front desk to inquire if they had rooms available.

"May I help you?" an employee asked.

"Yes, I would like to see if you have two rooms available for a one-night stay," stated Royalty.

The employee plugged the request into the computer and searched for rooms.

"Why yes," the employee stated, "we actually only have two rooms remaining for tonight. They are both smoking rooms and face the back of the hotel. A building obstructs the view from the window, so you won't have a view. Are you okay with settling for these two rooms?

"Yes, I'll take the two rooms," Royalty confirmed quickly.

The employee completed the check-in process and asked for the names of each person staying in the rooms. Royalty realized she didn't know the driver's name and decided to put both rooms in her own name. The employee collected payment from Royalty for both rooms and handed her the room keys. Royalty returned to the car to share the good news with the driver. However, she didn't see the vehicle or the driver anywhere around the hotel. Royalty searched the parking lot, but the car and driver were nowhere to be found.

Rest for the Weary

Royalty returned to the hotel lobby expecting to see the driver there, but she was nowhere in sight. At the front desk she asked the employee if she could leave the key for the driver. Royalty was embarrassed when the employee requested the guest's name and she had to admit she had no clue what it was. Royalty left a description of the driver instead, written on a sticky note.

> *"The driver is about five feet ten inches. She is wearing a black baseball hat, pink hoodie, black shirt, and black jogging pants. She has on white pearl earrings. She is quiet and reserved."*

These features were everything Royalty could recall about the driver, and she realized she might need to pay closer attention to the woman in the future—at least asking for her name in the morning.

Royalty hopped on the elevator and headed up to the sixth floor. The carpet in the elevator was covered by several brown stains. Some of its buttons were broken. The inspection notice needed to be updated, as it was last inspected eight years earlier. As the elevator crept up slowly to the sixth floor, Royalty was careful not to touch the walls. When Royalty exited the elevator at her floor, she smelled a musty odor in the hallway. This was not a place she would typically choose to stay. Luckily, Royalty's room was right beside the elevator. Royalty entered the room and was caught off guard by the smell of stale cigarette smoke. Though no one was currently smoking in the room, it smelled like years-old cigarette smoke had become embedded in the walls and furnishings. Royalty began to cough as her lungs reacted to the residual scent. She briefly sat on the bed and removed her shoes and socks. This was going to be a long night.

Royalty decided to shower as it might provide some needed relief for her lungs, even momentarily. She undressed and entered the shower. After attempting to adjust the temperature of the water for about four minutes, Royalty realized that the water was unlikely ever to heat up. She would have to settle for a cold shower. Royalty gave herself a quick rinse and then dried off.

In her haste to leave Peasantville, Royalty had left behind many items she needed now. She didn't have an extra set of clothes, her cell phone, or any toiletries. Luckily, she did have her ID, a bank card, and some cash.

After putting on her same clothes, she climbed under the blanket on the bed to warm herself and immediately drifted off to sleep.

About six hours later, Royalty awoke. She was disoriented but well-rested. She looked at the clock and noticed that it was already 10 AM. Royalty was confused because the room was still dark. She wondered if the hotel had dark curtains that prevented any light from seeping into the room. But when she opened the curtains, it was still dark outside. *Wow, where in the world am I?* Royalty wondered to herself.

Worry and the Book

Royalty had not heard from the driver for many hours and was becoming concerned. She picked up the phone and dialed the second guest room's phone number. No one answered. Now, Royalty was seriously worried. *What if I'm stuck in this town and this hotel? What if the driver left me? Where will I go? What will I do?*

Royalty began to tear up as the worry was consuming her. She decided to distract herself like she had before and searched through the drawers and cabinets in the room. Royalty opened the nightstand drawer and found a book with a worn surface there. Oddly enough, the book was simply entitled *The Book*. Royalty remembered hearing about this book before, but no one in Peasantville had access to it. Other peasants whispered about how people in other towns had access to it. The myth was that *The Book* was reserved for those with a special calling for their lives, so only they had access to it. That the peasants didn't feel a need *The Book* because they had figured out how to live their best lives and adhered to the same routines and standards.

Royalty contemplated grabbing *The Book* and holding it in her hands. By even holding this book, she knew she would be going against everything she'd been taught in Peasantville. However, Royalty figured she had nothing to lose at this point in her journey.

Royalty and lifted *The Book* gently out of the drawer. She was amazed at how thick and heavy it felt. Curious about its contents, she scrolled through *The Book*. It was a little challenging to read and understand the writing. But Royalty was stopped in her tracks by the following words: *The way of a lazy person is like a hedge of thorns, but the path of the upright is a highway.* Confused by their meaning, Royalty turned some more pages and was captivated by another sentence:

For God will give your angels charge over you to accompany, defend, and preserve you in every way.

At this point, she started getting goosebumps on her arms. Royalty had no clue what was happening but felt heavy from reading the words. Oddly, it was as if the words were speaking directly to her. She quickly closed *The Book* and put it near her room key so she would remember to take it with her. She was going to accept the label on the book cover that said it was free.

Royalty gathered her belongings and decided to wait for the driver in front of the hotel. *The driver must return,* Royalty figured. *That would be the only right thing to do.* She walked into the dense parking lot and looked around, but there was no driver or car. She sat down on a bench to wait.

After about an hour, Royalty grew weary. Her thoughts began to race again. Just as Royalty was again doubting her decision to leave Peasantville, she saw what looked like the Carolina blue car entering the parking lot. Royalty waved to the driver, who pulled around to the entrance. Royalty smiled and experienced a sense of relief that the driver had returned. The driver stopped at the front of the bench and got out of the car. She flashed a quick smile at Royalty and opened the back door. Royalty hopped into the car with *The Book* in hand and thanked the driver for her hospitality.

"What happened to you last night?" Royalty asked.

"I don't believe in limitations," stated the driver.

Royalty began to connect the dots as the driver headed off down the same highway. She was determined to make small talk today. "Thank you for coming back to pick me up."

The driver looked through the rearview mirror and uttered four simple words, "God cares for you."

Hearing these words, Royalty reflected on the lessons she had learned in the City of Limitations.

1. *Limitations are restrictive circumstances or self-imposed rules that obstruct us. We will all deal with limitations in our lives; however, we don't have to stay consumed by them or rest in them.*
2. *The City of Limitations has an unusually high amount of traffic. People tend to migrate toward spaces and places that put limitations on them. The path is familiar, and the expectations are modest.*
3. *The driver knows what is best for us. However, we have free will, which allows us to make decisions even if they are not best for us. When the driver tells you it is not the best choice for you, believe it.*
4. *Make sure to identify people by their names. However, to know their names, you need to have a relationship with them. Try to build relationships with people you share space with at work, at church, and in your neighborhood.*
5. *Don't get frustrated when other people choose not to stay with you in the City of Limitations. Some people have graduated from visiting this city.*

6. The Book *is an anchor that will help to keep you grounded. When* The Book *is opened and read, it causes anxiety and fear to be released.*

7. *The driver cares for you regardless of your decisions. The driver is always around, waiting for you to make up your mind.*

CHAPTER 6

The City of Hesitancy

Royalty and the driver were moving steadily down the highway. There was still no sun in sight. By now, Royalty had grown accustomed to driving in darkness and no longer questioned why there wasn't any light. Royalty realized that getting off the path and going to the hotel was not as restful as she had thought it would be. The hotel had been scary and was not comforting at all. What she imagined would bring her comfort was torment. The hotel did not provide peace, but *The Book* did. Royalty was grateful to have read a few of the sentences from *The Book,* and she even felt a little comforted by having it beside her in the car. But after everything she had been through, she totally forgot to ask the driver her name.

In the distance ahead, the moon appeared to be partially covered by a mountain peak that rose high into the midnight sky. Royalty scanned the horizon and wondered how difficult it would be for their car to drive uphill on such a steep slope. She found her anxiety and fear increasing again. Royalty had never been a fan of mountains, especially driving up and down them on twisting and turning roads. While Royalty was learning to trust the driver, she still felt discomfort in the prospect of going up this enormous mountain.

Because Royalty's focus was now entirely on the mountain, she missed a warning sign on the highway that read: CITY OF HESITATIONS.

Well Done

Royalty was caught off guard when the driver finally engaged her in a conversation lasting more than two or three words. "Are you enjoying your present journey?" she asked Royalty.

Royalty took a moment to get her thoughts together, then replied, "Not really, because I see the steep mountain ahead with sloping sides and high peaks."

The driver asked again, "Are you enjoying your *present* journey?"

This time, Royalty took a moment longer to reflect on what was being asked and how the driver put an emphasis on the word *present*. They hadn't reached the mountain yet, so their drive was still smooth.

"Actually, yes, I am enjoying my *present journey*," Royalty answered.

Royalty was astonished when the driver again smiled at her in the rearview mirror and said, "Well done."

Perhaps those words were supposed to comfort her, but as the car moved further toward the mountain range ahead, Royalty grew even more anxious than before. The driver continued driving them down the highway, and the car returned to silence. Royalty noticed that as they approached the mountain, the driver merged onto a different road, diverting them around the mountain peak and up a smaller hill. She realized that her focus and fears about the mountain had been premature and unnecessary. Royalty saw the mountain peak ahead, but the driver saw the path around this mountain.

Regaining calm as they drove up the small round hill, Royalty reached for *The Book* and flipped it to a section at the back. Royalty was captivated by the words: "Walk by faith, not by sight." As Royalty pondered this sentence, she realized that every time *The Book* was opened, the words spoke directly to her current situation. *This is odd*, Royalty thought.

She understood that this book was reserved for those with a special calling in their lives, so she couldn't understand how the book had landed in her hands as a peasant.

Uncertainty Arises

The mountain peak was behind them, but Royalty noticed another range of mountains straight ahead. She became a little anxious, but her fear subsided as she remembered there was a previous detour. This time, Royalty looked around to identify alternative routes or detours to avoid the mountain range. But she didn't see any, so she was beginning to panic again. Royalty thought she had avoided the mountains, but now she was surrounded by them with no way out. She could see, though, that the driver was relaxed and unbothered by the prospect of danger ahead.

Royalty never loved driving through mountains and would avoid such areas whenever possible. It always seemed that her car could go off a cliff at any moment. She felt as if she had less control when she was driving in the mountains.

The driver accelerated. The darkness lingered, and the mountains were ahead—a deadly combination. Royalty felt knots forming in her stomach. She braced for the road ahead and closed her eyes. Her mind was racing uncontrollably.

Royalty spoke her "final" words. "If something goes wrong, you can at least say you went on the journey," she stated aloud to herself.

"Maybe it's time I pray to Mighty God, the name I saw on the billboard. Maybe Mighty God can save me," she softly whispered.

"Mighty God, please keep us safe as we drive through these mountains."

The Mountain Cliff

Royalty kept her eyes closed so she wouldn't have to see the pending accident occurring. She began to hum the same tune that the driver had been humming earlier. As she relaxed and focused on the music, Royalty could feel the car moaning and spurting up the mountain. Twenty minutes later, she quickly glanced out of the corner of her eye to check their progress up the mountain. The driver was just pulling the car off to the side of the road and into a small parking area for mountain viewing.

The driver took the key out of the ignition and told Royalty to get out. But Royalty didn't want to get out and look over the edge of the mountain cliff. This did not seem at all relaxing to her. Plus, they still had to drive through the rest of the mountains. Resentfully and hesitantly, she opened the car door even so, and followed the driver to the viewing area.

Royalty noticed that the air at the top of the mountain was pure and crisp. She looked out over the view and saw pockets of lights on the horizon. Although the sky was dark, the view was astonishing. From the top of the mountain, Royalty wonders if she could see the final destination of the journey. Unfortunately, everything looked so far away, and it was just a mass of lights.

Royalty walked back to the car, uninspired by the walk. The driver entered the vehicle in a very peaceful and pleasant mood. "So, what vision did you have?" the driver asked.

"*Vision?* All I could see were the lights on the horizon. There wasn't anything else to see," Royalty replied rudely.

The driver asked the same question again, as if she was unsatisfied by the response.

Royalty didn't respond to the driver. She was beyond frustrated and tired of the repeated questions.

The driver maintained her pleasant demeanor, cranked up the car, and continued up the mountain. As the car motored further up the hill, Royalty's ears began to pop due to the elevation. She shook her head in disbelief that she'd ever allowed herself to get into the car to come on this "stupid" journey.

The driver asked Royalty once again, "What vision do you see?"

Royalty could not believe the driver was talking to her then, at the journey's most unsafe and inconvenient point. Royalty wanted the driver to focus on the road to keep them safe as they drove up the curvy mountainside. Although she had tried to carry on conversations with the driver a while before, now she was tightlipped. *This isn't how this works,* Royalty thought. *I control this conversation and relationship.*

Royalty decided to give a witty response to the driver. "*Vision?* All I have seen has been darkness for the last day and a half. Why don't you tell me what you see in this darkness? Do you have different eyesight or something? Do you see any light amid this darkness?" replied Royalty.

Royalty hoped her question would shut down the driver and end the conversation. Royalty was beginning to wonder if the driver was competent.

Interestingly, the driver remained calm and responded to Royalty with a smile on her face. "I am the light of the world," the driver said.

Realizing that the words from the driver were starting to sound like the words in *The Book*, Royalty decided to pursue this conversation further.

"So, I found a book in my hotel room, with some interesting words in it. Have you ever seen *The Book* before?" Royalty asked the driver.

"Yes, I have," the driver answered.

"It's weird," Royalty said, "how every time I open *The Book* and read a passage, it speaks directly to me."

Royalty noticed a slight grin on the driver's face but the driver still didn't offer a response.

"And though it seems to be speaking directly to me, I still can't quite understand what it means," explained Royalty.

Royalty looked at the driver's reflection in the rearview mirror, but silence prevailed. The driver still didn't have much to say. Royalty's patience was growing thin. *Why would the driver take me on this cross-country trip and not converse with me the entire time?* she wondered.

Royalty decided it was time to confront the driver about her behavior. "How come you won't say much more than a few words to me here and there," Royalty asked with a slight tone of frustration in her voice. Then she waited for an answer.

After a minute, the driver responded, "I've been talking the entire time, but you haven't been listening."

Royalty tried to understand what the driver meant. Reflecting on her time in the City of Hesitancy, she concluded:

1. *Hesitancy is being in a state of uncertainty and slow to act or intervene. Hesitancy is related to fear, self-doubt, and lack of trust. Its opposite is decisiveness.*

2. *Focusing on the present is where safety lies. It is not intended for us to focus on the future but to enjoy the present moment.*

3. *We may notice mountains and peaks, but the driver knows a detour. We shouldn't focus overly on potential obstacles ahead.*

4. *Sometimes we're so focused on the obstacles that we don't see the vision. Decide if you will keep your eyes focused on the obstacles or the vision.*

5. *Royalty never shared a vision because she didn't see what the driver was seeing. Don't miss out on vision because you are distracted by your own emotions and feelings.*

6. *The driver attempted to prepare Royalty to focus on the present before facing the mountains. However, she had difficulty staying in the present moment. Focus on the current moment. Don't fast-forward any problems in your life.*

7. *Focusing on the present allows you to see the vision. Royalty was unable to see vision because she was not focused on the present moment.*

CHAPTER 7

The City of Indecisiveness

Royalty reflected on the words shared with her by the driver. She had been in the car for almost forty-eight hours and thought she'd listened to the driver whenever they spoke. Royalty tried reflecting on the words spoken so far during the trip. Actually, they were so few and infrequent that there wasn't much to reflect on.

Royalty felt slightly insulted that the driver assumed she was not listening when she was sure she remembered every word muttered. Royalty challenged the driver with this notion as she noticed a sign ahead indicating they'd reached the City of Indecisiveness.

"I remember every word you said. You just haven't said much," Royalty said.

The driver smiled at these words and maintained her silence. After a few minutes in silence, which Royalty found painful, the driver opened her mouth again and stated, "If any person has ears to hear, let them hear."

Royalty was done communicating. In frustration, she abruptly ended what she perceived as a "wasted" conversation with the driver. The driver was speaking in riddles and needed to make more sense. The driver was starting to sound like the peasant minister. *Something must be wrong with this driver, maybe she's a little off in the head,* Royalty thought. She was glad the driver was only assigned to be her driver and take her to the final destination. She couldn't imagine spending the rest of her life with her.

Royalty was bored and getting weary in the back seat. She couldn't wait for the journey to be over. She glanced down at *The Book* beside her and fanned through the pages. She stopped towards the beginning of the book where she found the following remark: "God orders the steps of a good person."

Royalty liked the sound of this sentence. *Maybe, just maybe,* she thought, *Mighty God will order my steps.* She admitted to herself that at this point in her journey, it doesn't feel very orderly. In fact, the trip so far had been painful, challenging, and lonely.

Hey! Maybe if Mighty God can direct this trip, she will redirect this driver, so I can hurry up and get to the final destination.

An Unexpected Detour

Suddenly, Royalty noticed the car veering off the highway onto an exit ramp. The driver slowed the vehicle down and turned on her right turn signal as she patiently waited at a red light. The light changed and the car entered a new mega gas station on the righthand side of the road. The driver pulled over to a gas pump.

Royalty was relieved to have an opportunity to get out of the car and stretch her legs. She opened the door and heard her bones cracking as she rose from the back seat and stood close to the vehicle. She scanned the surroundings and was surprised to realize that every car at the gas station had both a driver and a backseat rider. Each rider looked worried and perplexed. Conversely, the drivers all looked the same: peaceful and calm. *This is weird,*

Royalty thought. *Are all these people on the same journey as me?*

Royalty noticed a pattern occurring. As many cars were leaving the station, the backseat rider smiled while the driver looked disappointed. As these cars left, they were heading in the opposite way on the highway, going back towards where they started.

Only a few vehicles continued going where Royalty and her driver were headed and with the driver and backseat rider demonstrating the same demeanors with which they entered the gas station. The driver appeared peaceful while the rider looked conflicted.

Royalty wondered to herself why most of the cars were heading back. *Is there something ahead that is unsafe for me? Is it better to turn around now?* Royalty sat back in the car and contemplated her options. *Life was so much easier before this trip.*

In Peasantville, Royalty didn't have to worry about where she was going or make significant decisions. Life was predictable. She didn't have to learn to trust a stranger and knew she could depend on her family and the peasant's view of God. When obstacles were faced, there were other peasants available to support her.

Royalty sorely missed home and the familiar. She was afraid of what might lie ahead. And her trust in the driver was dwindling. The driver wouldn't give her clarity about where they were headed. *What if I don't like the destination? What if the people there are weird, like the driver? What if I am lonely once I get there? What if I never make it back to Peasantville?*

The driver capped the gas tank, pulled the receipt, and jumped back into the car. Royalty got in too. The driver started the engine and quickly proceeded to pull out of the station.

Royalty wanted to turn around but didn't want to disappoint the driver. She didn't want her to think she had given up on the journey. On the other hand, Royalty couldn't imagine moving forward on this path. She was tired of this journey and tired of the unknown. She was tired of not being in control.

"I want to go back," Royalty softly admitted to the driver.

The driver shook her head in disbelief and left the gas station with the intent to head back down the highway toward Peasantville. Royalty looked at the driver through the rearview mirror and noticed a tear rolling down her cheek. *Why is she so disappointed?* Royalty wondered. *This is my journey, not hers.*

As the driver entered the highway, Royalty noticed that more cars were headed in this direction than the other. She also noted that the people in the back seat appeared smiling and happy. She felt a sense of relief and began to smile too.

Yay, I am headed back home, Royalty thought to herself. *I can catch up with my friends and family and let them know I am okay. I can return to my peasant church, job, and family. Oh, and I will update the peasant minister on the details of my journey.* Royalty was already experiencing a sense of peace and looking forward to her old comfortable and simple lifestyle. She had gone on the journey and was proud of herself for taking this significant step.

Brimming with joy and imagining returning to the familiar, Royalty leaned down to pick up *The Book.* Maybe I will hear some good news that will confirm my decision. *Perhaps Mighty God is looking out for me and answering my prayers.* Royalty turned randomly to a page and read the following passage:

"We also boast in our sufferings, knowing that suffering produces endurance, endurance produces character, and character produces hope. Now, this hope does not disappoint us because God's love has been poured into our hearts by the Holy Spirit, who has been given to us."

"Wow, people boast about suffering in this book," Royalty said softly to herself. "I suffered on this journey, but I couldn't imagine boasting about it."

"However, it is interesting that suffering produces endurance, and endurance character, and character produces hope. But who would want to deal with suffering to get to hope." She was speaking low so the driver couldn't hear her thoughts.

You Lead the Way

Royalty was startled when the driver spontaneously asked a question.

"How do I get back?"

"What do you mean?" Royalty said. "You drove me here, so surely you know how to take me home."

"It's different," the driver stated, "when you are the backseat driver, you oversee your journey and lead the way. You tell me where to go, what highways to take, and what hills to climb. You direct the journey. It's my job to drive the car and stay by your side to ensure you get where you think you should go. When you are the backseat driver, I become the rider in your journey."

Royalty was bewildered. She had ignored the route on the way there and trusted the driver. Plus, it was still dark outside. Royalty needed help figuring out how to get back home. As the rider, she had learned to trust where the driver was taking her and allowed herself to lead. Now that the journey was in her own hands, she didn't like the thought.

"You don't know how to get me back to Peasantville?" Royalty asked the driver.

"No, I'm responsible for taking people out of bondage, not putting them back into it," the driver responded.

"And you don't know the highways or directions back? Can't you pull over and ask for directions?" Royalty inquired.

"No, I only know the way to growth, prosperity, and abundance. I don't ask for directions back to bondage or know how to return to Peasantville. I choose to stay by people's side when they journey back because I know the pain they will experience and I don't want them to experience it alone. But asking for directions back to bondage goes against my nature," the driver replied.

Immediately, Royalty felt a heaviness in her spirit that she had never felt before. *Is Mighty God showing up to me at this moment?* Royalty thought she might be experiencing the presence of Mighty God but wasn't sure.

Royalty felt more and more distressed. Royalty mentally replayed the last forty-eight hours she had spent with the driver. While the journey was unknown and the driver had only limited interaction with her, she had developed a sense of comfort during the trip. Royalty had constantly experienced new paths, highways, and mountains on this journey. Now that she was headed back to Peasantville, nothing was new. She knew she would experience the same people doing the same things. Was this what she really wanted? Was she willing to trade long-term misery and discomfort for a temporary experience of joy at returning home?

Royalty was indecisive and trying to figure out what to do next. She contemplated her next move and saw there was a new city limits sign ahead. Before reaching it, she pondered what she had learned in the City of Indecisiveness.

1. *Indecisiveness is the state of being unable to make decisions effectively and quickly. Although Royalty made the decision to leave Peasantville, and also to return to it, she was still stuck in a state of indecision. She needed to feel more confident about her decision making.*
2. *The driver was decisive and always knew the appropriate route to take to pursue her purpose and destiny.*
3. *We have to be willing to endure suffering. Suffering produces endurance, character, and hope.*
4. *The driver allowed Royalty to make decisions about her next move. Despite her choices, the driver never left her side.*
5. *When we take a different path than God has intended for us, the driver will stay with us. We can trust that the driver won't ever direct us down a path of destruction.*

6. *Life continues as we sit in our indecisiveness. We must have the courage to make decisions that align with our purpose.*

CHAPTER 8

The City of Tragedy

Royalty began to imagine how happy she would be to see friends and family. At the same time, she accepted that happiness would be short-lived. She wondered if there was a way to have the best of both worlds. While reflecting on these issues, Royalty saw a sign reading TRAGEDY CITY LIMITS.

Suddenly, Royalty was startled by a loud, crashing noise ahead on the highway and jerked her head toward the source of the noise. In disbelief, Royalty saw that one car had smashed into the highway railing and two more in a ditch.

"Oh no," Royalty yelled, "I hope they are okay."

The driver remained calm and pulled off to the side of the road. Upon a quick glance, the extent of the damage to the car on the railing signaled that there wasn't much hope for the people that had been riding inside it. Royalty and the driver raced, along with a few others, to the crashed vehicle. When they arrived at the site of the accident, they saw a bloody mess. There was a backseat rider in the car that had hit the railing, a woman about forty-five years of age. The passenger appeared to have been crushed on impact and died. Royalty was distraught by the goriness of the scene.

Upon first look, Royalty realized that there was something familiar about this passenger. She walked around to the other side of the car to catch a better glimpse of the passenger's face. In utter shock, she realized who it was: her former neighbor, Faith. *OMG. What was Faith doing on this highway? Why did she even get into the car? She would have been safer staying in Peasantville,* Royalty thought.

Royalty maintained faith in the well-being of the other passengers in the cars stuck in the ditch. But as she hurried to these cars, she discovered that they too were both crushed from impact. The onlookers were able to remove the backseat riders from the vehicles. Royalty then moved closer and saw their faces. Royalty lets out a brief shriek of recognition. One passenger was an associate from Peasantville named Hope.

The other was her friend Joy. *No, this can't be. Why did these individuals die so tragically? Why didn't they both stay in Peasantville?* Royalty felt incredibly discouraged. She wondered if her friends were looking for her on the highway. Perhaps they had learned that Royalty left in a car with a stranger and were attempting to locate her. Until this sighting, Royalty had no clue they had also taken this journey. Had they been following her? And did her decision to return to Peasantville have something to do with their own decisions to return?

Royalty started to take blame for all three deaths.

Now, this definitely has to be a sign that I need to return to Peasantville, she contemplated. *This journey is unsafe and not worth risking my life. One major wreck caused fatalities, and they were all in cars on their way back to Peasantville.*

Royalty took small steps as she made her way back to the car. She was distraught and at a loss for words. Royalty acknowledged that all of those who died were in the backseat of vehicles at the time of the accident.

Where Are the Drivers?

Something clicked in Royalty's mind. *There were no drivers in the front seats of the three cars. What happened to the drivers? Did the drivers abandon their passengers? Did the drivers intentionally wreck the cars and leave these people behind them to die?* Royalty stirred with anger. Her confusion was increasing by the moment.

Royalty looked around to find her driver so she could ask her some questions. She wanted to get to the bottom of what was going on because someone needed to be held responsible. Royalty spotted her driver speaking to some other drivers. Oddly enough, they were all reasonably calm mannered despite the recent accident.

The Journey Will End

"Can we talk for a minute?" Royalty whispered into her driver's ear.

"Sure," the driver answered and walked away from the other drivers with Royalty.

"What happened here? Where are their drivers, and why are all these backseat riders dead?" Royalty inquired.

The driver looked Royalty directly into her eyes and spoke in a low tone. "The drivers were no longer needed in these situations. Each passenger's time had come to an end," she stated.

Now Royalty needed clarification. "Why were the drivers no longer needed?" Royalty asked.

"The drivers in those cars did all they could to support the passengers on their journeys. The drivers knew that each passenger's journey had a designated start date and end date. Because the drivers knew the end dates, they tried to steer the passengers in the right direction. But the drivers allowed the backseat riders to have self-determination and make decisions they felt were in their best interests. Sometimes a journey ends before a passenger can reach their final destination on earth. And often, a journey ends with the backseat rider returning to their hometown and ending their journey early," the driver solemnly said.

"However, rest assured," the driver stated, "the driver stays with the backseat rider until no more life is in them. They then depart that car and find another to work out of. They go back to work, taking a new passenger on the journey."

Trusting the Driver

Royalty awakened. She now understood why the driver was trying to keep her on the journey.

"The good news for your friends," the driver said kindly, "is that just because they didn't finish what amounts to a spiritual journey before they died, and just because they experienced a tragedy, doesn't mean they won't ever finish their journey. Sometimes the journey is cut short so that a driver can carry them toward the destination sooner than expected. Only a few individuals actually will reach the final destination while here on earth."

Royalty walked over to say her final goodbye to her friends. She started with Faith, her neighbor. "Faith, you didn't spend much time at home, as you loved working at your church and in the community helping with any needed tasks for hours. As much as you sacrificed, you often neglected to prioritize your own needs. Faith, thank you for teaching me about sacrifice and the importance of investing in myself."

Next, she moved over to Hope. "Hope," she said, "you taught me about the gift of contentment. Every time I would see you, you had a broad smile on your face. You were always happy: happy with life, happy to be loved, happy to serve. You taught me how to be satisfied with what I had, nothing more and nothing less. And everyone who was around you was blessed by your presence. You had a way of shifting the energy in any room. I will miss your sweet spirit."

Lastly, she moved to Joy to say a few words. "Joy, you taught me about the gift of perseverance. You were a beacon of light here in our world. Your works blessed so many people. Although you suffered from physical concerns that caused you tremendous pain and discomfort, you persevered and maintained your joy and hope. Perhaps you embarked on this journey because you desired something more for yourself. Thank you for your deposits of joy in others' lives. I'm sorry your life had to end tragically like this."

She realized that Hope, Joy, and Faith decided to take the same journey, and knew that, like herself, they had decided to return home, although it didn't end well. The gifts they left behind were sacrifice, contentment, and perseverance. Maybe they had left them to encourage her. Perhaps this was what she needed to finish her journey.

Royalty walked over to the driver. In silence, they stood and waited by the wreckage until tow trucks came to haul away the damaged vehicles, and ambulances carried away the bodies. Then she hopped into the backseat and wasted little time informing the driver that she wanted to turn around again and continue her spiritual journey.

Royalty refused to give up now. She was determined to move forward with the trip to honor the memory of her friends.

With a smile, the driver whipped the car around and headed them back on route for the ultimate destination. Royalty took one last look back at the site of the accident over her shoulder and whispered goodbye.

As she was reflecting on what she learned in the City of Tragedy, Royalty cried. She understood:

1. *Tragedy is any event that causes us physical, mental, or emotional distress and suffering. We*

will all experience tragedy at some point in our lives; although no one finds tragedy a desirable experience, it is possible to draw something positive from enduring it, such as lessons about the strengths of perseverance, love, resilience, and compassion, among others.

2. *When we stray from our journey and try to return to Peasantville too soon, we will only experience momentary happiness. We may open ourselves up to harm if we go off track.*

3. *There comes the point in your life where you must make the pivotal decision to head towards your final destination. The journey will be worth it. Although you may feel alone, the driver will always be with you.*

4. *As a passenger, learn how to submit to the driver and allow the driver to lead the journey.*

5. *What appears to be a tragedy is also an opportunity to position people so they may fulfill their purpose and experience freedom.*

6. *You are connected to people who will share the gifts you need for your journey. Receive these gifts. Others are connected to you because of the gifts you will give them. Give freely.*

7. *When a loved one dies, you may receive gifts from them. What gifts have you received?*
8. *The driver knows the end date of your spiritual journey. Trust when the driver encourages you to continue traveling. Be confident in your decisions.*

CHAPTER 9

The City of Doubt

Royalty was contemplating the last few hours of the ride and shaking her head. She couldn't believe she had initially decided to take the "easy way out" and chosen what was comfortable. At the same time, she was grateful that she had the opportunity to say some parting words to her three friends. Had she not turned around to go home, she would never even have known they had died. It could be that the return was meant to give her a chance to spend those moments with her friends, not to give her a chance to return to Peasantville.

Now she was sitting in the back seat on her way to the destination again. Royalty had finally accepted that it was easier to sit there and trust the driver. But to trust the driver, she would need to build a relationship with her. She admitted to herself that she knew very little about the woman. For instance, she still didn't know her name, where she was from, or how she had ended up as a driver.

Now was the time for Royalty to learn to trust her driver more. But then she saw a sign ahead that they were entering the City of Doubt.

It Sounds Like a Fairytale

Royalty contemplated what to say to the driver to break the awkward silence in the car. Not feeling very creative, she asked, "So, where are you from?"

The driver looked in the rearview mirror with a slight upturn of her lips. Royalty could tell she was pleased to be invited to engage in a more substantial conversation.

"I am from a place called Freedom City. You've probably never heard of it," stated the driver.

"You're right. Please tell me a little about your city," said Royalty.

"Absolutely," the driver said with a sparkle in her eyes. "Freedom City is a place of peace, faith, happiness, joy, and love. It is an island that produces the best crops: fruits and vegetables better than you have ever tasted. Sunshine glistens on white sand and warms the clear, shallow waters of the ocean around the city. It is a place where there is prosperity and overflowing resources. In this place, there is no weeping, crying, pain, or suffering because everyone has all their needs met. There is no scarcity or mediocrity. Everything is done in excellence."

Royalty was suspicious about the existence of such a place. She had doubts that it existed on earth. She had never heard of anything like it before. In Peasantville, people sometimes spoke about a place like this, but everyone believed it was reserved for life after death.

"I don't understand how this place can exist on earth. It sounds like a fairy tale. Is this a place you dream about or somewhere you have been yourself? This can't be a real place. I've never heard of it before," stated Royalty.

The driver continued offering her description in a relaxed state and didn't allow Royalty's doubts to hamper her excitement. She recognized Royalty's skepticism for what it was.

"In Freedom City," the driver said, "the struggles in life are no more, and everyone is considered family. We all help each other out and are focused on the same purpose. We aim to help bring other people to this city to experience abundant life.

"I was specially assigned as your driver. You were appointed to be on this journey and experience freedom while on earth. However, I can't make you go. I can only support you along the way. My heart longs for you to make it to Freedom City and reside there. However, you need to have more faith in me and in yourself. You simply cannot have doubt to complete the journey," the driver shared.

Being known by her community in Peasantville as a person of faith, Royalty was offended by these comments. She had always had faith. Royalty knew the formula for praying to God. She prayed whenever she wanted. All she had to do was ask God for what she needed and wait to see if he answered.

And she knew all the hymns the peasants sang. She also donated money weekly to the collection plate at church. Royalty always did everything "right" and was never a doubter—until now.

This talk from the driver was blasphemous!

"In Peasantville, I always had faith and I have been the one person in my family who was always willing to trust God," said Royalty.

The driver remained calm and said, "It's easy to have faith in Peasantville where not much is expected from you. But this journey is a true test of your faith. Your doubt causes you to return to Peasantville when things get difficult. Doubt causes you to avoid building a relationship with me. Doubt causes you to consider yourself more holy than you are. Doubt causes you to be too proud. Faith dismantles pride; however, it requires work."

Hearing these words, Royalty was speechless. Was it easier to maintain faith in Peasantville? Is that why she had previously wanted to return? Was she dealing with the issue of heartfelt pride?

The driver's words stung and Royalty didn't like how she was feeling. She found herself questioning her character and intentions. If getting to know the driver would cause her such discomfort, did she really want to get to know her? Royalty was not ready to deal with her character issues. She had been perfectly comfortable before with not having to address any of these sorts of issues.

Royalty decided the conversation was over. She also felt tired from hearing her internal dialog. She slowly nodded off with her head pressed against the headrest and her eyes blindly staring out of the side window at a blur of passing scenery. Initially, she fought against falling asleep, but the battle was soon lost.

There was much for her to learn in the City of Doubt, including the following.

1. *Doubt is a feeling of uncertainty or not knowing what to do or believe.*
2. *You cannot trust the driver and hold on to doubt simultaneously.*
3. *When there is an effort to trust the driver, doubt will attempt to return. You have to fight to push through it.*
4. *When you develop a relationship with your driver, you discover more about yourself. Some of what you learn will be comfortable, and some will be uncomfortable. Develop the relationship anyway.*
5. *Character work can be difficult and tiresome.*
6. *Trust is the opposite of both doubt and pride.*
7. *It's easy to have faith when you have low or mediocre expectations. Raise your level of expectations for yourself and Mighty God and watch your faith increase.*

CHAPTER 10

The City of Storms

Royalty woke from her nap in the backseat to see the windshield wipers streaking across the car's windshield at a super high speed. Crashing thunder seemed to shake the car as bright, flashing lights illuminated the sky. Suddenly, hail rained down in golf-sized pieces that beat against the car roof. These were pounding so heavily on the vehicle that it was tough to see the road ahead.

"Do you need to pull over?" asked Royalty, wanting to let the driver know it was okay for them not to rush to their final destination in this weather.

"No, it's just a storm," the driver stated calmly. "It's important to learn how to travel through storms. Besides, you are not alone. You have a driver, and there is nothing to worry about."

As the driver finished this remark, a massive bolt of lightning flashes across the dark horizon. Royalty was afraid and didn't feel protected in the car. This was the worst storm she had ever seen.

The driver continued driving at the same speed.

"Would you please slow down and pull off at the next exit?" said Royalty in a demanding tone of voice. "I've never been in a storm this bad, and I'm not sure we will be able to make it safely to the destination."

Without saying a word, the driver immediately pulled the car over to the shoulder of the road instead of pulling off at an exit. Royalty wondered if maybe the driver was irritated with her.

"How come you didn't go to the next exit? What is the point of just sitting here in the storm?" asked Royalty.

"You must learn to manage the storms of life. You can't always run to safety or your favorite place of comfort. You must learn to handle storms and sit through them patiently. It's uncomfortable, but your growth happens in the storm. For amid the storm, you learn where your soul is anchored."

"Your soul should not be anchored in a car. It should not be anchored in your circumstances. And it definitely should not be anchored in your abilities. It must be anchored in Mighty God. The storm forces you to anchor yourself in Mighty God, who becomes your place of safety. When you are anchored to Mighty God, you are at your safest," stated the driver.

Forced to Stay in the Storm

Royalty was a runner. She was used to leaving situations and circumstances when things became difficult. She preferred maintaining control and exiting situations whenever she was ready to leave. This had become her way of coping with life. "Why sit around and deal with hardships when you can easily escape them?" she always said. It made no sense to her to wallow in pain or a difficult situation or to make space for spiritual uneasiness in her heart. Royalty would instantly cure her uneasiness by running away; it worked every time.

Right then, Royalty was being forced to sit and endure the storm. She couldn't talk her way out of it because the driver wouldn't listen. Royalty herself wasn't driving the car and she didn't have the key. Therefore, she was stuck: no running, no way out.

Royalty sat quietly in the car, feeling startled every few minutes by the sound of the lightning and rolling thunder. Each minute, the thunder seemed to get closer to their location. And they just sat there and waited.

There was dead silence in the car. All the noise was outside it. Royalty glanced up to see if the driver had fallen asleep but noticed she was peacefully gazing out of the window at the environment. *How can the driver feel at peace during such a violent storm?* Royalty wondered.

As Royalty's trepidation from sitting unprotected in the midst of the storm increased, she looked down and saw *The Book* lying on the floor beside her foot. She reached down and picked it up, then scanned the pages. Royalty stopped at a page where she was taken aback by the words she read.

"You will neither fear the terror of night, nor the arrow that flies by day, nor the pestilence of the plague that destroys at midday. A thousand may fall at your side, ten thousand at your right hand, but none will come near you."

The words in *The Book* always seemed to speak directly to her situation whenever she opened it. Royalty's eyes zoomed in on the word *fear*. She remembered that fear was an emotion or feeling caused by the belief that something would not work out. She had already passed through the City of Fear. Could that again be something with which she was dealing? She had to acknowledge that she was experiencing fear as she sat through this storm and found herself believing that things would not work out the best for her.

Royalty had always considered herself bold and courageous, as those were the traits by which her family and friends always described her. However, had she only been brave and courageous because she was in Peasantville? Did she know how to be bold and courageous outside her comfort zone?

As Royalty reflected on this question, she accepted that she had relied on comfort more than courage during this trip. Sure, she had decided to get into the car, but she had never resolved to fully experience the journey. She realized that she had yet to fully embrace and experience the journey. She also pondered whether she had perhaps attempted to recreate Peasantville in her car experience with her driver.

Leaving your comfort zone doesn't mean you take it with you. It means you leave it behind. When you take it with you, it stagnates your progress.

You're Not Alone on the Journey

At that moment, Royalty committed to releasing herself from fear. She realized that her approach to this journey and the experiences involved in it needed to change. Each day and hour of this journey must have her full attention. Royalty wanted to be fully aware of the meaning of the signs she saw so that she could keep progressing.

She remembered what the driver had said about enjoying the present moment, and realized that her protection in this car came from this driver.

She also acknowledged to herself that she couldn't hope to make this journey alone. She didn't have the competence, capacity, or ability to reach their final destination without relying on the driver. And she confirmed, also to herself, that she was inviting Mighty God into her journey. Royalty reflected on the driver's message about having an anchor. From then on, she would anchor herself to Mighty God.

Royalty summarized the many lessons she learned in the City of Storms.

1. *Storms are violent disturbances in any atmosphere containing strong wind, rain, thunder, lightning, hail, or snow. Key to this definition is that the storm is a temporary disturbance—a brief interruption. Storms don't last forever.*

2. *The Book commanded Royalty not to live in fear and promised that the attacks would not come near her. She was protected from the storm by being in the car. The storm couldn't get directly to her since the driver and the car protected her.*

3. *Royalty was afraid because she didn't think it would work out based on her abilities. She had yet to trust the driver.*

4. *You can't make the journey alone, because you need the presence of the driver to reach the final destination.*

5. *To abolish fear and push through the storm, stay in the present and be grateful.*

The City of Peace

Altogether, the storm lasted about twenty minutes, and then the driver merged back into the traffic on the highway, and they were headed towards Royalty's final destination. They continued in silence, as was their custom, with the driver driving at an accelerated pace.

Royalty saw a small ball of light in the sky. She figured that she must be closer to her destination because she was seeing golden rays of sunshine illuminating the clouds. The sun was rising and the darkness finally ending.

Royalty blinked her eyes repeatedly to focus her eyes which had grown accustomed to the dark. The car was driving over a high, arching bridge that crossed over a large body of crystal blue water. This water was the prettiest water Royalty had ever seen. It glistened as the rays of the sunrise touched its surface.

Royalty had always wanted to see the ocean, but like most people in Peasantville, she had never left town to experience anything different. *This must be our destination*, she thought. *It's so beautiful.* But as they crossed the bridge, she saw a green sign that told her otherwise. It read: PEACE CITY LIMITS.

Royalty glanced at the driver, who appeared to still be in her own little world, smiling and enjoying the ride. *How can the driver be so happy, peaceful, and joyful all the time?* Royalty wondered. *And what else does the driver do with her life? Does she drive people around every day? Does she have a family?* Royalty had so many questions that she doubted she would ever get them all answered.

Royalty wanted to talk to the driver, but only if the driver would provide honest answers and feedback that did not hurt her feelings.

Lack of Clarity and Lack of Relationship

Royalty noticed the driver looking at her in the rearview mirror.

"How are you enjoying the ocean?" the driver asked with a broad grin.

"It is amazing—literally the most beautiful thing I have ever seen," Royalty replied.

"How come you still aren't enjoying it?" asked the driver. "The living waters flow continuously, but you have to awaken yourself to them."

Royalty was furious because she had no clue what the driver meant. How did the driver know that she wasn't focusing her attention on the ocean?

"Do you want a relationship with me or not?" asked Royalty. "Or is it your goal to confuse me on this trip and bring up everything that's wrong with me and how I do things?" She was adamant about getting straightforward answers to her questions this time.

"You only lack understanding of the things I say to you because you don't know me well yet. Once you get to know me better, everything I say will make sense to you. Your confusion is due to your lack of investment in our relationship until now. My words are helping you to acknowledge your need for me. But your doubt, fear, and lack of trust are making it difficult for you to develop a deeper relationship with me—and this is making you feel frustrated," the driver said.

"So, how do I get to know you better? I've asked you questions, but you tend to provide limited responses. You haven't engaged with me much at all," Royalty said, imagining that her words might stump the driver.

"You listen and pay attention. I speak directly to you with my voice, as well as through other people and through nature, but if you do not listen or pay attention, you will miss the majority of these messages," the driver stated.

Royalty knew she had never been the best listener. She was used to other people coming to her for advice and being able to quickly produce a good solution. Royalty wasn't expected to listen much as she often had the best answer for people. Being still and listening just seemed like a waste of time given her ability to solve problems.

"If you would have listened closely, you would have heard how the ocean was speaking to you." the driver said. "But you were distracted, so you missed out on that conversation."

Peace Abounds

Okay, this is getting weird, Royalty thought. *How does an ocean talk?* Royalty decided to stop asking questions, as there was no point. She got quiet and enjoyed the beauty of the ocean. She saw small birds crossing over the ocean. She saw the waves gently rising and falling as they crawled toward the shore. She opened the window, breathed in the salt air, and closed her eyes to listen to the sounds the ocean made. Royalty could hear the mighty waves of the ocean crashing up against the bridge they were driving over.

Royalty heard peace in the ocean. Its rhythm reminded her of being held and rocked in her mother's arms. As Royalty listened to the ocean, a phrase her mother used to recite came to mind.

"God makes you lie down in green pastures and leads you beside quiet waters."

Her mother's words echoed in her head. Royalty had never understood this phrase as a child but now that she'd had an experience with quiet waters it made more sense to her. Royalty silently repeated the phrase several times as her eyes remained closed. And she felt a peace transcend over her that she had never experienced before. She didn't know where this sensation was coming from, only that it felt good. She never wanted to let go of the experience.

After a few moments, Royalty opened her eyes and saw that the car had passed the ocean. She wondered how long it had been since they finished crossing the bridge. The driver looked at Royalty in the rearview mirror and smiled again. This time Royalty smiled back.

Finally, Royalty felt safe, protected, and at ease. She had agreed to fully immerse herself in the experience of the ocean and was proud that she had followed through.

The ocean was amazing. Royalty contemplated the lessons learned as they were traveling through the City of Peace.

1. *Peace is freedom from disturbance and tranquility. We should expect to feel peaceful, particularly following a storm.*
2. *After going through storms, you will experience amazing peace. You have to travel through the storms to get to peace.*

3. *Mighty God speaks to us via multiple methods. Try deliberately paying more attention to hearing directly from nature.*

4. *When going through a season of peace in your life, don't try to rush the experience. Allow yourself to fully enjoy and revel in the peace. Allow your senses to engage in the experience.*

5. *The driver will attempt to refocus you on the season of peace when you get distracted.*

6. *Don't forget to be grateful for the season of peace. Demonstrate your gratefulness by allowing yourself to fully immerse in it.*

7. *The driver desires for you to fully experience a peace that transforms all understanding.*

CHAPTER 12

The City of Surrender

Royalty panicked when she noticed red lights on the road ahead of them. The car slowed down and merged into the right lane.

"Please don't let this be another tragic accident," Royalty mumbled under her breath.

The car came to a stop. The entire highway was like a massive parking lot. Royalty saw four black cars with red sirens blocking the highway in front of them. Cars were waiting patiently in the right lane and inching slowly past the congested area. From the procession of vehicles, it looks like each car was stopping for an assessment and then, once approved, it was able to proceed. These vehicles didn't look like police cars.

After inching forward for about twenty minutes, Royalty and her driver finally arrived at the checkpoint. They could see that four individuals dressed in all-black clothing were speaking to the driver of each vehicle that pulled through.

The driver of her car rolled down the window. She no longer had a smile on her face. This was the most serious expression the driver had worn during the entire trip.

"Can you give a report on the progress of your backseat passenger?" the stranger asked the driver.

"Yes, this is Royalty Jones. She has come from Peasantville and is ready to pursue her purpose. Together, we've made it through the Cities of Fear, Limitations, Hesitancy, Indecisiveness, Tragedy, Doubt, and Storms. We only turned around one time on the journey. She has reflected on the lessons she learned in each city. She has started reading *The Book* and listening to the word. She also experienced peace traveling through the last city," proclaimed the driver.

"Interesting, another member of the Jones family. I haven't seen one in years," the stranger said. "It sounds like she has endured and overcome the challenges in the easy part of the journey. Has she developed a relationship with you?"

Hearing this question, Royalty felt nervous. She still didn't know her driver's name or much about her. And honestly, she hadn't fully believed everything the driver had told her.

"She is beginning to develop a relationship with me," stated the driver.

"But does she know your name?" inquired the stranger.

"No, she doesn't know my name," admitted the driver.

Appearing disappointed, the stranger asked the driver, "Will you allow her to continue the journey to the next town?"

"Yes, I will offer her my grace and mercy. She can continue to the next town," the driver said confidently.

"Is she aware of what lies ahead?" the stranger asked the driver, patiently waiting to hear her response.

"No, she is not aware, particularly since she doesn't know my identity, but she is learning to trust me," the driver said.

"Okay, you can proceed," stated the stranger. He looked at Royalty, smiled, and then said these parting words: "The driver's grace and mercy is what is allowing you to proceed, not your own work or efforts."

Royalty was already aware that she didn't know the name of her driver. But she had not known until now that she would need the grace and mercy offered by the driver to continue her journey. She felt immensely grateful to the driver. She realized that she would need her more than ever.

The driver locked eyes with Royalty in the rearview mirror and nodded her head. Royalty nodded back to her in appreciation.

Focusing on the Driver

As they moved forward, Royalty was momentarily distracted by the city limits sign for the City of Surrender. She felt extremely fearful again. *What is going on?* she wondered. *What lies ahead, and how come my driver didn't prepare me for this phase of our journey?*

The driver pressed heavily on the gas pedal and accelerated the car past the roadblock. As she did, Royalty experienced paralyzing fear. The storms they had persevered through so recently were terrible enough. What else would she have to endure on this journey?

Royalty looked out of the window helplessly. A tear ran down her right cheek. She wanted to trust the driver, but the journey had made her tired. She had hoped that her troubles were over once they entered the City of Peace.

Royalty handled her disappointment by focusing her attention on the driver. Perhaps now would be a good time to initiate a conversation with her. Royalty was ready to build a deeper relationship.

As Royalty contemplated how to attempt this next conversation, the driver turned on some music. Royalty loved the melody and listened closely to the lyrics.

I surrender all to you.
Everything I give to you.
Withholding nothing.

Royalty had heard about surrendering at her church back in Peasantville, but always believed that surrender was mainly for weak-minded people. As she listened to the song, Royalty decided that the lyrics didn't apply to her. Perhaps the driver liked this song and just wanted to play it to hear the melody. Royalty chose to proceed in engaging in small talk with the driver.

"Is this one of your favorite songs?" Royalty asked the driver.

"Yes, how did you know?" the driver replied, laughing. "It's such a beautiful song. It talks about how we must surrender and allow Mighty God to have control of our destiny. Hearing the song reminds us to give Mighty God everything we have and not to hold on to things we want to control ourselves," she explained.

"Well, I like the music, but the lyrics don't apply to me. I've never felt the need to surrender to God fully. God already exists within me and has a place in my heart. And the things God blesses me with I use to bless others. God has blessed me with too much to let go of everything," Royalty said.

The driver quickly responded, "The problem with most people is that pride makes them think they have things under control. Surrender is a way to commune fully with God by letting God know that you will depend on, lean on, and trust God 100 percent, rather than on your understanding of the world and events. It is a way of saying, "I trust you with no conditions attached.

"Surrendering to God doesn't mean the road gets easier. It means that when you follow your purpose in life you have God ahead of you, somewhat like having me as your driver. With a driver for your life, you don't have to worry about where you are heading, what's on the road, or the storms you could face. A trusted driver takes you on the best path available."

"When you don't surrender to God, you are essentially making yourself into a god. You are telling God to go along with *your* plan. For example, think about when we attempted to return to Peasantville and you felt as if you needed to lead the way. Did you know where to go? How to get back? More importantly, when things became difficult on our journey, who led you safely to the next town? Was it you or me?

"God wants to take you toward your purpose, your destiny, but you must let God drive you there. And not just driving some of the time, but all of the time. God doesn't need you ever to switch seats and assist with the driving. God wants to drive you the entire way. That's what *withholding nothing* means," explained the driver.

The Need to Surrender

The message finally seeped into Royalty's mind: She thought more highly of herself than she did others. Her pride was causing her to believe that specific principles didn't apply to her. It clicked that she needed to surrender. She had not made it this far through her own might and will. The journey was being made with the help of the driver.

Royalty realized that as time passed, she had increasingly focused on the driver and focused less on the journey. And as she learned to trust the driver more, she heard more from and could more clearly understand the driver. The driver's role was now starting to make sense.

"So, how many people have you taken on this journey?" Royalty inquired.

"Honestly, I have lost count of how many people I've attempted to drive while they were here on earth. Everyone is invited to take this same journey. But most people end up making the journey only after they die."

"Well, that's weird," said Royalty. "Why wouldn't they want to make it to the final destination before dying?" she asked directly.

With a tinge of sadness in her voice, the driver replied, "Many people have learned from religion that they can only reach the final destination *after* death. So, they experience bondage in Peasantville for their entire lives. And I am always sad when those that leave Peasantville decide to give up, return, and never try again because the journey is too uncomfortable for them, or they lack patience. They have not learned to develop a relationship with the driver and enjoying the journey of getting to the final destination."

"So let me make sure I understand," said Royalty. "You're saying that many people begin this journey but never make it to the destination. And because they are only stuck on reaching the final destination, they miss out on developing a relationship with the driver and the process. Why is that?"

"Some never dare leave their homes to begin the journey. Others start the journey but don't reach the destination due to a lack of faith. They also lack a desire and willingness to develop a relationship with their drivers. They simply don't think they need a driver. Some can't deal with the process of returning to Peasantville only to begin the journey again. They believe they have failed and give up hope. They fail to acknowledge the lessons they have learned along the journey.

"As a result of turning back and staying in Peasantville, they stay in bondage. And often they judge people who attempt to make the journey. They laugh at those who end up turning around and mock them. Sometimes they even oppress them and assign them to a lower social status.

"Although few people on earth have made it to the final destination, those who do will experience transformative joy, peace, and love. After taking the journey, they can't imagine living on earth without the experience of inner, spiritual freedom," explained the driver.

Royalty realized that turning back and living among the peasants in Peasantville likely was why her family had a lower social status than their neighbors and were oppressed. As she had begun to suspect, members of her family took the journey before her. She reflected on the passed-down stories of relatives who tried but failed to make it to the final destination. Her family had accepted these stories as legends.

Royalty appreciated the courage and boldness of her ancestors for deciding to leave Peasantville but realized she didn't know anyone who had completed the journey.

In Peasantville, people were led to believe that you could only make it to the destination after death. But the driver was informing her that, in fact, the opportunity was an option while living on earth. Most importantly, people's success on this journey was based on their relationship with Mighty God, not their work, deeds, or social status. They needed to experience God.

She finally asked a question she had been eager to ask for a long while and did not have the courage to ask before. "What is your name?"

"I thought you would never ask. I revealed my name to you early in the journey, but you overlooked it. My name was revealed to you on the first billboard that we passed on our journey through the City of Fear," said the driver.

Royalty remembered the billboard and repeated the words written on it aloud: I AM THAT I AM— MIGHTY GOD. In utter shock, Royalty let herself digest this new information for a moment. She quickly acknowledged that her expectations of Mighty God had been based on peasant expectations and the teachings of her religion. She had expected Mighty God to look and sound different than she did. She expected Mighty God to show up more as a judge. She didn't expect Mighty God would be her driver.

"Wow, I always thought God was a man," she whispered to herself. "Now I realize that God is a spirit displaying both masculine and feminine qualities."

She hadn't expected Mighty God to actively work to develop a relationship with her or to drive her to her final destination herself.

Feeling like nobility, Royalty expressed her gratitude. "Thank you for being my driver on the journey. I'm sure you had other people you could have chosen to drive, so I thank you for choosing me. You inspire me to keep going, and I appreciate that," she said.

The driver grinned at Royalty again, and Royalty noticed a twinkle in her eyes. The driver was taking note that Royalty had finally recognized her identity as being more than a driver.

"Now, I am her friend," Mighty God whispered under her breath.

Royalty was excited to reflect upon the wisdom she learned in the City of Surrender. She noted that she had learned the following lessons.

1. *Surrender is choosing to submit to the authority of God and give up our personal agenda. To make it to the destination, surrender is required. We need to allow God to direct our path.*

2. *Prior to entering the City of Surrender, the driver had to vouch for Royalty and give an account of her progress. Despite how good we think we are or how much progress we've made on our own, surrender requires us to acknowledge our needs.*

3. *We have to acknowledge that can't do it on our own.*

4. *Every day, God gives us grace and shows us mercy.*

5. *The journey is about developing a relationship with the driver more than it is about reaching the destination.*

6. *Many people are afraid to take a spiritual journey. It takes courage and boldness to be willing to pursue the final destination.*

7. *Mighty God wants to be your driver and is ready for you to accept the ride.*

8. *Mighty God is not confined to our perceptions. Mighty God is so much bigger than our perceptions.*
9. *Mighty God wants to support you and be your friend. Mighty God desires a relationship with you.*

CHAPTER 13

The City of Freedom

As the car rounded a curve, a sign ahead read: FREEDOM CITY LIMITS. Royalty thought that this might be their final destination, although it was seemingly quite familiar. She waited for the driver to announce that they had arrived, but it didn't happen. Looking out the window, Royalty expected to see stunning views and a luxurious city. She imagined there would be large mansions nestled into beautiful, rolling hills. But none of that was the case. As they entered the town, it was familiar, and perplexing, because it looked as if they were back in Peasantville. She pondered, *Why did I go on the journey if I was returning back to the same town?*

She waited to see if she would be greeted by friends, family members, or even strangers. But this is not the case. This destination did not meet her expectations. The City of Freedom was Peasant-ville. Was this a joke or a test? A tear rolled down Royalty's cheek. Her disappointment in this long-awaited destination was immense.

"My friend," said Mighty God, "what are you crying for?"

Royalty was too upset to tell Mighty God what was on her mind. She was beginning, yet again, to lose faith in her. Royalty sulked in her seat and disconnected from the driver. There was a palpable chill in the air between them. Royalty had had enough of the games.

Mighty God continued cruising through the town, passing familiar streets and landmarks. Royalty got confused when Mighty God turned down a side street and then a bumpy gravel road leading to the peasant minister's church.

"Where are we going?" Royalty yelled at her. "First, we make it to the City of Freedom, which is really just Peasantville. And now, you're taking me to the peasant minister's church? What is going on? I need answers, NOW."

Mighty God maintained her silence and continued driving down the gravel road to the parking lot in front of the church. The tension in the car thickened.

Finally, after parking, the driver spoke. "Residence in the City of Freedom requires one to exist in a higher, more spiritual state of being. It is not merely a destination. We actually arrived in the City of Freedom after you began to trust me, Mighty God, because you were ready to develop a relationship with me and we became friends. But although we had physically arrived, you never arrived spiritually. Arrival in the City of Freedom is a spiritual matter.

"I would love for you to experience freedom fully. However, spiritual freedom requires you to remain in a consistent state of surrender. You must trust in me to stay free.

"I have longed for you to make it here, and my grace and mercy allowed you to physically arrive. However, you are not yet ready or willing to trust me, surrender fully, and have faith in me. You are still more willing to maintain your doubt, comfort, and control. As a result, it feels like you are in Peasantville. To feel your freedom, surrender.

"Peasantville is a city of freedom, love, prosperity, faithfulness, and kindness to those who engage and commune with me in an ongoing relationship. They can continue to reside here, yet their experience is transformed into something heavenly.

"To reiterate: To commune with me, you must be ready—fully ready—for this experience. You must stay connected to me and trust me wholeheartedly. There must be a transformation in your mind and spirit.

"Once you accepted me as your friend, I became your permanent driver. While I am disappointed that you still do not fully trust me, you have not lost my favor. I love you just as much as I did before this experience. I love you despite your imperfection, doubt, pride, and disbelief. Nothing you can do will make me love you any more or any less. My love for you is unconditional. I love you, my friend.

"From now on, I will always be your driver. I will never leave you, but I am waiting for you. I will be here to take you on other experiences with me when you are ready spiritually. Your relationship with me will develop once you let go and allow me to drive—meaning, when you allow me to design your experiences according to my will."

Royalty felt disheartened. As much as she wanted to continue the ride, she understood that she was not ready to go further yet. She knew that she had not fully developed unwavering faith and trust in her relationship with Mighty God.

As they conversed in the car, Royalty and Mighty God learned more about each other. She got more information about Mighty God's partners, the other drivers. Each was responsible for transforming people's lives and developing deeper relationships with them through sharing divine experiences. She learned that no one can be truly transformed without grace and mercy from Mighty God or one of her partners.

Royalty and the driver exchanged stories from their pasts, including memories from this trip. They laughed and bonded like old friends.

Their conversation was interrupted when the peasant minister knocked on the driver's side window. Mighty God quickly opened the door and left the car. She gave the peasant minister a huge hug as if they were best friends who hadn't seen each other in years. There was a special bond between them.

Royalty got out next and greeted the peasant minister with a hug.

Mighty God shared details about the journey with the peasant minister, including news of towns they had visited.

Hearing about their adventures, the minister said, "I am so proud of you, Royalty. You took the journey with my friend, Mighty God, and made it through so many towns on your first ride. That is impressive for a first-time rider. There are an infinite number of cities you could visit, and you made it through ten of them. As you passed through each, you experienced something greater and more refined. You experienced miracles, signs, and wonders of all kinds. And, best of all, you traveled through the cities with the driver leading the way. The journey is a profound experience."

"But what about the final destination?" inquired Royalty, still trying to understand how to get to the end of the journey. "Is the City of Freedom the final destination?"

"There is no final destination," said Mighty God. "The relationship with me is ongoing and neverending. The journey is an experience that continues as long as you allow me to be your driver.

I will take you through different cities, depending on my needs and my will for your life. And sometimes you will end up in the same place you started, just experiencing it as a different person. There is so much work to be done in Peasantville, but I need you transformed to carry out my will. Regardless of where your experience with me takes you in the future, the focus is more about surrendering and trusting me and allowing me to do a good work in you."

Following these remarks, Mighty God said goodbye and quickly departed to pick up her next backseat rider.

Watching the driver leave, a tear rolled down Royalty's cheek. But in a weird way, she didn't feel alone.

Looking into the eyes of the minister, Royalty expressed her gratitude by gently saying, "Thank you for introducing me to your friend. My life will never be the same."

"Absolutely," stated the minister. "Remember, I am that I am. You have made us proud."

Royalty smiled and walked towards the oak tree, the place where her experience with God began.

CHAPTER 14

Lessons from the Driver

As Mighty God drove away from the church, she reflected on the lessons she learned throughout the journey that she wanted to share with backseat riders in the future.

1. *You may not understand your royalty. I have sent people to remind you that you are not a peasant, even if you feel comfortable existing as one. Ask yourself, "What do I enjoy about being a peasant?"*

2. *Some people have awakened to their innate nobility. These people lead lives full of love, joy, peace, patience, kindness, goodness, faithfulness, gentleness, and self-control. They see open doors and are willing to walk through them. On a daily basis, they commune with me, acknowledge my presence, and listen for my*

voice speaking to them. Have you awakened to your innate nobility? How do you imagine you will know when you have awakened?

3. *Unfortunately, many people die never knowing their identity as a spiritual being or their innate nobility. Some die never having experienced greater possibilities.*

4. *In life, you may choose either comfort or growth. You are at a critical point in your life. If you are riding in my car, you won't always be comfortable but you will be growing. No matter what, you can trust me and depend on me wholeheartedly.*

5. *You are not fulfilling your purpose when you stay in your comfort zone. This begins to separate you from me. It hurts me to see you live beneath your potential because you are choosing to be comfortable rather than trust me and have a relationship with me. Are you choosing comfort over our relationship? Are you choosing to live a mediocre life void of my presence?*

6. *When your identity is thoroughly grounded in the truth of who you are, you will embrace my full identity as Mighty God.*

7. *Fear may be the sole factor preventing you from advancing to the next level of spiritual development in your life. It's important to acknowledge that your fears exist but not to allow them to stagnate you. Often, fear creates an illusion of comfort in your current circumstances. You believe things are going great because you are not being challenged or growing. Lack of growth equals comfort, and this is a result of fear.*

8. *Messages are sent to you as soon as you can handle them. They may not make sense today, but they will return when you need clarity with life events.*

9. *I will always be the driver of every car. I may not appear to you as you expect me to look, but I am present. Commune with me and have a conversation. I want to get to know you more intimately.*

10. *Surrender is about the willingness to have trust, faith, and obedience. When you are willing to operate in trust, faith, and obedience, you can enjoy the City of Freedom.*

11. *Feeling lost? Then read The Book for precise directions.*

CHAPTER 15

Lessons from the Backseat Rider

Back at home, Royalty lay on her bed with *The Book* and a journal in hand. She said a brief prayer to Mighty God and then wrote down some lessons she had learned during her journey.

1. *The first step to surrendering is saying yes. Mighty God will not force you to say yes but creates circumstances to encourage you.*

2. *Mighty God is waiting to take you to greater places. You have to be willing to trust her and take the journey.*

3. *The world has created an image of God with limited power. This God makes life comfortable by maintaining our low expectations. Eliminate this perception and seek Mighty God who has all power.*

4. *The car is all about positioning. The driver needs you to remain in the back seat and ride to truly experience a state of total surrender.*

5. *Achieving a state of complete surrender allows you to experience freedom. You will get to experience heaven here on earth.*

6. *Tragedy will strike, but it doesn't mean you won't reach the final destination. The tragedy is a detour to getting someplace greater more quickly.*

7. *Expect to encounter storms and steep mountains during your journey. But understand that just because you see mountains ahead doesn't mean you have to climb them. Mighty God will sometimes provide you with a detour.*

8. *Mighty God is not a respecter of persons. God does not believe that some people are more deserving than others. Everyone on earth gets an opportunity to ride.*

9. *Mighty God does not conform to our visual expectations. Eliminate biased perceptions of how Mighty God will look or sound. Mighty God can show up in any identity and in any place. Mighty God can also show up in nature.*

10. *Many of us will search for Mighty God without realizing that God was with us the entire time, driving our car. Mighty God needs us to be sensitive to her presence.*

11. *We will fail many times on this journey. When this happens to you, don't be discouraged. Start the process over. Try again. Mighty God provides grace and mercy and will allow you to continue your journey because God cares for you.*

12. *Surrendering means having the courage or willingness to trust Mighty God. You must let go of your need to be in control and be willing to trust.*

CHAPTER 16

Lessons from the Minister

When the minister returned to his office in the church, he reflected on the lessons he learned from this experience.

1. *Mighty God has declared royalty among the people but people have to awaken to their nobility.*

2. *There are people connected to each of us that are assigned to intercede on our behalf before, during, and after our journeys.*

3. *When you have been on a journey with Mighty God, your change. You may not fit in with the same people and places as before.*

4. *After you have journeyed with Mighty God, she will surround you with people who are able to understand and appreciate your journey.*

5. *Mighty God is approachable and relatable. We can build a relationship with Mighty God.*

6. *When you spend time with Mighty God, you gain wisdom. People may not understand your advice and guidance but offer it anyway.*

7. *Freedom is a spiritual state of mind. As a child of Mighty God, you are entitled to live in freedom, but this requires you to accept it.*

8. *I am a minister for the peasants but not a peasant minister. I know my purpose.*

RESOURCES

Sonyia Richardson, Ph.D.
Another Level Counseling & Consultation
3210 Prosperity Church Road, Suite 101
Charlotte, North Carolina 28269
(704) 548-5298
SonyiaRichardson.com

Engage with Dr. Sonyia Richardson

Dr. Richardson is available for consulting and speaking opportunities.

Keynote and Workshop Speaking

As a sought-after speaker, Dr. Richardson delivers transformative talks for small and large groups. She has worked with several Fortune 500 organizations, churches, and nonprofits, providing various content. She is applauded for her depth of knowledge, wisdom, and experience.

Video and Audio Products

Dr. Richardson has an impressive social media presence and delivers her series "Your Online Therapist" to audiences internationally. The series is free and focuses on increasing access to a therapist for individuals around the globe. In under one minute, Dr. Richardson provides a message for the work to help listeners with personal growth and development.

Organizational Consulting

Dr. Richardson works with consultants in her practice to provide directions and innovative solutions to organizations to help support their overall success. Under Dr. Richardson's guidance, she and her consultants offer tailored services to meet specific organizational needs.

Concierge Coaching

Dr. Richardson provides selective coaching and development to leaders internationally. She focuses on helping them to learn how to show up fully, align with growth principles, and tackle fear and anxiety.

Sonyia Richardson, Ph.D., is a healer and motivator, encouraging others to live bold and courageous lives. An entrepreneur and therapist for over fifteen years, she owns Another Level Counseling and Consultation in Charlotte, North Carolina, a company that seeks to transform lives through holistic healing. As a professor and researcher, Dr. Richardson is teaching and training the next generation of healers while developing innovative interventions to meet diverse mental health needs.

Dr. Richardson was named 2021 Social Worker of the Year by the North Carolina National Association of Social Workers. She earned a doctorate in curriculum and instruction from the University of North Carolina, Charlotte, a master's degree in social work from the University of North Carolina, Chapel Hill, and a bachelor's degree in psychology from the University of North Carolina, Charlotte.

A member of Alpha Kappa Alpha Sorority, Inc., Dr. Richardson is passionate about helping others to pursue their purpose, justice, entrepreneurship, and life transformation. She also enjoys spending time with her spouse, Rondell, and their two sons, Micah and Jayson.

www.ingramcontent.com/pod-product-compliance
Lightning Source LLC
Chambersburg PA
CBHW060458300726
48975CB00008B/2551